THERE IS NO DOG

Praise for *How I Live Now*

'A crunchily perfect knock-out of a debut novel' – *Guardian*

'This is a powerful novel: timeless and luminous' – *Observer*

'That rare, rare thing, a first novel with a sustained, magical and utterly faultless voice' – Mark Haddon, author of *The Curious Incident of the Dog in the Night-Time*

'Intense and startling . . . heartbreakingly romantic' – *The Times*

'A wonderfully original voice' – *Mail on Sunday*

'Readers won't just read this book, they will let it possess them' – *Sunday Telegraph*

'It already feels like a classic, in the sense that you can't imagine a world without it' – *New Statesman*

Praise for *Just in Case*

'A modern *Catcher in the Rye* . . . written with generosity and warmth but also with an edgy, unpredictable intelligence' – *The Times*

'Unusual and engrossing' – *Independent*

'Intelligent, ironic and darkly funny' – *Time Out*

'Extraordinary' – *Observer*

'Rosoff has an eye so sharp and turns of phrase so apt that you can't forget them' – *Toronto Star*

Praise for *What I Was*

'Rosoff's most perfect novel . . . It's already a classic' – *Sunday Times*

'Thrilling and sensitively told' – *Observer*

'This exquisitely written novel, complete with amazing twist,
is the "teenage" book of the year' – *Irish Times*

'A wonderfully warm, witty, intelligent and romantic story
with a terrific whiplash in the tail. Textured, nuanced,
dramatic and atmospheric,
What I Was feels like a future classic' – *Daily Telegraph*

'Gently haunting' – *Metro*

'Compelling and all-encompassing . . . Sucks the reader
whole into its universe' – *Time Out*

'One of the best plot twists in a novel to be found this year'
– *The Herald*

'In her compassionate, honest meditation on the human condition,
Rosoff takes us places no one else can'
– *Toronto Star*

Praise for *The Bride's Farewell*

'Exhilarating . . . Every sentence is crafted and weighted with beauty'
– Amanda Craig, *Times on Saturday*

'An engaging, impeccably written novel'
– *Independent on Sunday*

'A poetically charged romance, full of thorny emotional dilemmas . . .
compelling' – *Marie Claire*

'Rosoff's writing is luminously beautiful' – *Financial Times*

'A wildly inventive romantic adventure' – *Red*

'It's not often that one comes across a book as richly detailed
and layered as this . . . perfect' – *Daily Telegraph*

'A highly polished gem' – *The Scotsman*

'This exquisitely written journey into freedom, love and womanhood makes literature out of the pony tale' – *The Times*

'*The Bride's Farewell* is a book that lingers in the mind' – *Irish Times*

'Pure Rosoff' – *Guardian*

Praise for *There Is No Dog*

'A wild, wise, cartwheeling explanation of life, the universe and everything. Given the glorious, eccentric, spectacular cock-up that is Planet Earth, the Creator can only have been a slack, male adolescent with a short attention span and an unruly sexual organ. I don't know why no one has worked this out before. It makes a whole lot more sense than particle physics. And, unlike Big Bang Theory, it's funny' – Mal Peet

meg rosoff

THERE IS NO DOG

DOUBLEDAY CANADA

Doubleday Canada and colophon are registered trademarks

Library and Archives Canada Cataloguing in Publication

Rosoff, Meg
There is no dog / Meg Rosoff.

ISBN 978-0-385-66831-6

I. Title.

PZ7.R719563Th 2012   j813'.6   C2012-902358-2

Cover design adapted from a design by Natalie C. Sousa
Cloud images courtesy of Shutterstock.com
Printed and bound in the USA

Published in Canada by Doubleday Canada,
a division of Random House of Canada Limited

www.randomhouse.ca

10 9 8 7 6 5 4 3 2 1

To Paul and Sally G,
without whom there
would be no dog.

When his life was ruined, his family killed, his farm
destroyed, Job knelt down on the ground and yelled up
to the heavens, 'Why, God? Why me?' and the
thundering voice of God answered, 'There's just
something about you that pisses me off.'

Stephen King

1

Oh glorious, most glorious glorious! And yet again glorious!

The sun spreads warm and golden on Lucy's face and arms. Pale new leaves unfurl so fast she can almost hear the little sighs they make as they open. Birds tweet and twitter their social networks, like city workers seeking potential mates. A few tipsy clouds punctuate the sweet blue sky. The world reels, drunk with happiness.

Lucy nearly laughs out loud. What a wondrous day. The most wondrous day ever, since the very beginning of time.

She doesn't realize how much she herself adds to its perfection. Is it the summer dress printed with roses, which the breeze catches and flips up against her legs? Or merely the fact that Lucy is as perfect as a rose herself, a flower newly opened – so perfect, you can imagine the sun breaking every rule of impartiality to beam down upon her, alone.

What heaven, she thinks. What bliss! Whoever is in charge of the weather today has (for once) achieved perfection.

Her step is light. The distance from bus stop to work is short. She smiles, a half-grown girlish womanish smile that illuminates her lovely features. The sun paints soft highlights on her cheekbones and well-shaped mouth, sets her pale hair alight. She dreams about the summer months to come, the bright conversations, the long pink evenings, the possibility of love. Her youth, her smile, her happiness all combine, at this moment, to make her the most irresistible woman on Earth.

A young man walks some distance behind her. If he hadn't already made up his mind not to fall in love – with her or anyone else, ever again – he might run to catch her up. Instead, he slows his step and turns away, disliking her, for not very good reasons of his own.

Lucy fairly skips along, joyous. She passes a fountain and leans over into the spray, delighted by its sparkling rainbows. Then she straightens and resumes her walk, humming a little prayer, which is not so much a prayer as a hope, a private incantation: '*Dear God*,' she prays, '*I should like to fall in love.*'

But wait . . . what's this? Such luck! God (who almost never bothers listening to his people) overhears her prayer. Lucy's prayer!

Transported by her loveliness, he decides to answer it himself.

What a miracle! How much more than glorious! God, himself, is about to fall in love.

2

'Wake up!'

God is dreaming of water. In his dream there is a fountain, and a naked girl, and (of course) there is him. The water is warm, the girl willing; her flesh is soft. He reaches out a hand to caress her breast, curls his fingers instead round one slim arm . . .

'Wake. Up.' An edge of impatience accompanies the request.

Oh, Christ. It's that dreary Mr B – his assistant, private secretary, God's very own personal bore. And surprise surprise. B's spectacles have slipped down to the end of his nose and he has his sourpuss face on.

God is awake. He cracks open one eye. '*What?*'

'Go to the window.'

His head hurts. 'Just tell me.'

'Get up. Feet on the floor. Walk to the window. Look outside.'

With a huge sigh, a brain thick and slow as pudding, the boy sits up, swings his legs on to the floor, stands, sways for an instant and runs one hand through his hair (which he can tell, with annoyance, has all migrated to one side of his head, as if he's been standing in a high wind). Groaning, he turns and pads wearily to the window, his feet bare and cold. The rushing noise is louder than it was. To his surprise, there is water where the streets used to be and for a moment he feels quite relieved that his bedroom is not on the ground floor of the building. 'Water,' he says, with interest.

'Yes, *water*.' Mr B's manner is mild, but he trembles with unexpressed feeling.

God struggles to make sense of the scenario. Why is there water in the streets? Did he make this happen? Surely not. He's been sleeping.

'Look over there.'

He looks.

'What do you see?'

Off the bedroom is a large bathroom, complete with toilet, sink, white marble tiles, large rolltop bath.

Bath.

The bath! God remembers now; he was running a bath and then, as he waited for it to fill, he lay down. Just for a moment. He must have fallen asleep. And while he slept, dreaming of that beautiful girl, the girl in the fountain, the bath overflowed.

'Oh.'

'Oh? Just *oh*?'

'I'll turn it off.'

'I've turned it off.'

'Good.' The boy heads back to bed, collapses.

Mr B turns to God with his customary combination of resignation and rage. 'I don't suppose you'd like to do

4

something about the mess you've made?' Outside the window water rolls through the streets.

'I will,' he mutters, already half asleep. 'Later.'

'Not later, *now*.'

But God has pulled a pillow over his head, signalling (quite definitely) that there is no point going on at him.

Mr B fumes. God is dreaming of soapy sex with his fantasy girlfriend while the rest of the world drowns in the bath. His bath.

It is always like this. Day after day, year after year, decade after decade. And on and on and on. Mr B (more than a personal assistant, less than a father figure – a fixer, perhaps, facilitator, amanuensis) sighs and returns to his desk to go through the mail, which (despite being dealt with on a daily basis) has a tendency to pile into vast teetering towers. He will choose one or two prayers and make an attempt at urgent action. He does not show them to God, for the boy's ability to concentrate is minimal at best.

Occasionally a voice leaps out from the torrent of prayers and moves him by simple virtue of its sincerity. *Dear God, I should like to fall in love.*

An undemanding little prayer. From just the sort of sweet girl he would like to help, in the first place – by making sure God never lays eyes (or anything else) on her.

But God has a bloodhound's nose for a gorgeous girl, and before Mr B can hide the prayer the boy is out of bed and peering over his shoulder, snuffling at the prayer as if it's a truffle, practically inhaling it in his anxiety to get his hands on . . .

'Who is *she*?'

'No one. A dwarf. Short, hairy, old. A troll. She grunts, she snores, she stinks.'

But it's too late. He's seen her. He watches Lucy in her thin summer dress as she walks through the dappled morning light – *his* light – her round hips swaying, her pale hair aglow. She is exquisite. Flawless.

At that exact moment, there is a blinding flash of light. It is so intense that for a moment the world disappears.

'I'll have her,' says God.

When Mr B manages to open his eyes once more, the expression on God's face makes his heart sink. It is twelve parts moony love, eighty-three parts sexual desire, and ten and a half million parts blind determination. Oh, *please*, Mr B thinks, not a human. Not *another* human.

He is filled with despair. God's passion for humans always leads to catastrophe, to meteorological upset on an epic scale. What is wrong with the boy that he can't get it up for some nice goddess? Why, oh why, can't he pursue a sensible relationship, one that will not end in disaster?

Mr B could weep. Attempting to talk God round is as useful as trying to reason with a squid. He will pursue Lucy until his lust wears out, or until some vast geological disturbance erases her from the Earth. Mr B has seen it all before. Earthquakes, tsunamis, tornadoes. God's unique inability to learn from his mistakes: yet another wonderful trait he's passed on to his creations.

Happy now, the boy drifts back to bed, where he dozes, conjuring filthy scenarios around the girlfriend he hasn't yet met.

3

In the beginning God created the heaven and the earth.

Only it wasn't as simple as that. The preferred candidate for God withdrew at the last minute saying he wanted to spend more time with his family, though privately everyone suspected he was having second thoughts. You couldn't really blame him. Earth was badly positioned – miles off the beaten track in a lonely and somewhat rundown part of the universe. At a time of high employment, not many top-level candidates were willing to take on a tiny unproven planet, not to mention the whole creation rigmarole, which, when done properly, could be a real headache.

The job posting had attracted barely a handful of candidates – most too young or too old, the rest so under-qualified that they never made it to interview. The only serious applicant, a middle-aged man known as candidate B, had a solid but unexciting record in middle management; when he appeared before the board to state his credentials, his quiet, somewhat professorial manner failed to generate enthusiasm. Agreement could not be reached.

The hours ticked by. With a deadline upon them, the committee required a decision. But the administrator was going through a messy divorce, and the team that should have been sorting out Earth's management was busy with other projects. The final day of the tender arrived with no one to take the position. Tempers frayed, minds wandered and at last one of the board members offered the job as part of a bet on a not very good game of poker. The player who won, promptly turned it over to her feckless teenage son. Bob.

Bob's credentials (non-existent) did not impress. But the general sense of exhaustion and indifference was such that no one could really be bothered to argue. And, anyway, he might turn out to have great potential. Stranger things had happened.

What swung the deal at last was the suggestion of a sort of coalition – between the unproven son and that stuffy old codger, Mr B. It being so late in the day, everyone expressed enthusiasm.

'All in favour?'

The motion carried. Bob's mother informed him of his excellent good luck and B was told to jack in his current job and prepare for transfer. Two of the governors took him aside and explained his role – he would, they said, have a good deal of responsibility, given how inexperienced the other appointee was. 'We think you'll work well together.'

The fact that the job had not gone entirely to Mr B was a terrible blow, final confirmation that the career ambitions he had treasured quietly over the years had come to nought. Had he been too introspective, not ruthless enough? Had he been wrong to assume that years of competent, responsible service would attract notice?

The sinking feeling that Mr B experienced at his first meeting with the new boss did not augur well. The boy was arrogant, badly brought up and monosyllabic, patently uninterested in sharing the job and unembarrassed by his general ignorance. Mr B had been around long enough to know that start-ups were tricky operations, not to be bartered casually in poker games or entrusted at random to someone's chippy know-nothing son.

Oh well, he thought. If the boy fails, it'll be his problem, not mine. But in his heart Mr B knew this was untrue. If things went well, the kid would get all the credit. If not, he, himself, would get the blame. He hoped the committee would be proved right about Bob – hoped his energy and creativity would somehow make up for what looked, on paper, like a lamentable lack of experience. Mr B shut his eyes and hoped against hope that somehow it would all turn out fine.

He had lived long enough to grasp the danger of hope.

4

Lucy enters the zoo through the employee turnstile.

She has worked here three months and, though it is not a particularly large or sophisticated zoo, she loves it dearly, considers herself among the very lucky to have landed such a job.

'I shouldn't be telling you,' whispered the human resource manager, 'but more than ninety people applied.'

The team that runs the zoo consists of just two senior keepers and six juniors. They specialize in families and school groups and have only last month received a commendation for services to education. An environment this intimate resembles a family and, in the manner of all families, the zoo is not without its petty politics. But Lucy is not attracted to trouble, and wakes up every morning delighted with her lot.

All of this she considers as she changes into her blue overalls and hauls the metal zip up and over her chest, pushing a stray lock of hair behind one ear.

'Hello, Luke.' She addresses the senior keeper, a bit nervously. 'Shall I start on reptiles this morning?'

'Your call,' he answers briskly, without turning to look at her.

Luke is the flaw in Lucy's happiness. At first she thought he might be shy, or perhaps socially awkward. But lately she has noticed that he seems perfectly able to share a laugh and a drink with just about anyone but her. She is not the sort of girl accustomed to making enemies, and it is a point of private puzzlement that his face, when he looks at her, is stony.

She is not to know that her appointment irritated him greatly. He feels certain that if he'd been involved in the hiring process, one of the other applicants would have triumphed – for surely her good looks trumped more qualified candidates.

On this basis, he has made it his policy to avoid her, determined not to be suckered into her circle of admirers. Positive reports of her performance he discounts as motivated by infatuation, a sort of mass hypnosis among the staff. One slip, he thinks (ignoring an accumulating pile of evidence that she might, after all, be quite good at her job), one slip, and he'll insist that they replace her with someone proper.

'Good morning, beauties.' Lucy aims her greeting at a wall of glass vivaria as she unlocks the door to the reptile kitchen. She wrenches the heavy freezer lid up and pulls out a frozen block of embryonic chicks, placing them on a metal tray to thaw. 'Breakfast,' she murmurs, with a little grimace. 'Yum.'

In the first glass box, she lifts a sixty-centimetre corn snake aside gently and scrapes out his soiled bedding with a trowel. The bulge in his neighbour's stomach from yesterday's mouse is still visible. The boa can be churlish while digesting, so she leaves him, moving along the row to update feeding charts. She pokes at the thawing chicks with a fork; three or four minutes in the microwave will sort them out.

Lucy loves snakes, loves the sensual skim of them against her skin, like silky leather. She doesn't love defrosting their meals, but on balance it's a small point. At least the monkeys, God bless them, eat fruit.

By the time she has finished reptiles it is mid-morning. She is desperate for a cup of coffee. Emerging into the bright spring day, she blinks rapidly; her pupils shrink and for a moment the world darkens. When she can see again, she looks left and right, a little anxiously. It has become a habit, she realizes, one that annoys her greatly – this seeking to avoid Luke.

The coast is clear and she crosses over to the staff room, which at this hour is nearly empty. Oh, please let there be coffee in the pot, she thinks, but there is none. And so she rinses it, removes the old filter and sets about making fresh, glancing at her watch as she fills the machine. She has time, just, to get the monkeys fed by lunchtime.

Lucy hears voices, and turns to see Luke and his assistant, Mica, passing the window. They are laughing together and she freezes against the wall like a rabbit, hoping to make herself invisible. *Don't come in*, she prays, and slumps a little with relief when they don't.

How is it that he makes me feel guilty about a cup of coffee, she thinks angrily. Like I'm skiving? Like I make a habit of bunking off work?

She fetches milk from the fridge, trying to view Luke objectively, to imagine what others see in him – entirely without success. Mica thinks he's good-looking but Lucy can't see it. With that personality? The coffee machine pings.

She pours, adds milk and gulps it down as quickly as possible. Oh well, she thinks, a little ruefully, I suppose that's life. And anyway, things change. He could get a new job tomorrow, move on, find some other innocent hard-working employee to dislike for absolutely no good reason at all.

Draining her cup, she rinses it and runs a sponge quickly over the worktop. Back to the grind, she thinks, and despite herself she laughs. What a dimwit I am. Best job in the world and all I can think of is the flaw.

As she steps out into the light, Bob watches her, shivering with devotion.

5

Bob's talent, such as it is, consists entirely of the few unconscious charms of youth: its energy, audacity and complete inability to recognize its own shortcomings.

Mr B has means to cope. Routine, for instance. Every day begins the same, with two slices of rye toast, unsalted Normandy butter, raspberry jam, two poached eggs, strong coffee. And for the boss, at whatever hour he happens to wake, hot tea and half a box of Coco Pops. Bob's pet stands by the edge of the table willing food to tumble off into his mouth. He is an odd penguiny sort of creature with the long elegant nose of an anteater, beady eyes and soft grey fur. The Eck is always hungry; no quantity of leftovers can fill the eternal emptiness of his gullet.

From Bob's room, Mr B can hear thrashing and sighing. Since the discovery of Lucy, God has slept fitfully, unable to escape the iron jaws of sexual desire. The transformation from needy teenager to weapon of mass destruction is nearly complete.

Eventually he wakes. With a sigh, Mr B gets up from his desk and carries tea to Bob's bedside because it is his job to do so.

'It's noon, sir.'

'Oh, *sir*, is it?' He's cranky. 'Wasn't *sir* yesterday, was it?'

'The flood?'

Bob screws up his face and farts. '*Your* job is to know in advance that I'd forget to turn off the bath.'

'Eck?' Eck looks from Bob to Mr B, hoping for a fight.

But there will be no fight. The older man may not accept responsibility for the calamity, but Bob does not actually care.

God pouts. His thick adolescent hair has fallen over one eye, and his skin has the greyish tinge of someone who doesn't leave the house often enough. Yesterday's bath would have done him good.

'Your clothes, O Holy Master of All.' Mr B bows and hands him a sweatshirt with a large sporting-goods logo on it, which Bob dutifully pulls over his head. He hasn't changed out of the same T-shirt in what might be a week now.

'Any progress on the girl?' He tries, and fails, to sound casual.

'None at all, nothing, nada,' says Mr B. 'Doesn't know you're alive, as far as I can tell.'

'*Why* doesn't she know I'm alive?'

Mr B can feel a strop brewing. He feels obliged to assist Bob in every endeavour – but not unduly, not enough to complicate his own miserable existence. He sighs. 'Why not be upfront about it, let her know you're up for a bit of squishy woo-woo and see what she says?'

A look of quite superior contempt suffuses the boy's features. 'She's not the sort of girl you can get into bed as easily as that.'

Oh really?

'Can't *you* tell her?' Bob's contempt dissolves to oily supplication. '*You* can make her like me. I know you can. You've done it before.'

'Not any more,' Mr B answers. 'I've resigned from pimping. It's not in my job description.' In point of fact, he has no job description, or if he ever had, it was so long ago that the details have been lost in the mists of time.

'I can *make* you help me.'

The look of petty menace on the boy's face makes Mr B shudder. It is difficult for him to imagine that any woman finds Bob attractive.

'Go out and tell her how you feel. Or you'll end up wanking alone in your room till the end of time. The worst that can happen is she rejects you.' He knows this to be particularly cruel, for rejection is what the boy fears most.

Bob looks glum. 'How do I find her?'

'Zoo. Tuesday to Sunday, 9 a.m. to . . .'

The noise that emerges from God's mouth resembles a wail. 'I never know what to do in one of those animal places. How do I get in? What do I say? *What if she doesn't like me?*'

'Buy a ticket. Visit the hippos.'

Bob storms out and slams the door. He feels beleaguered. In the old days, they wouldn't be having this discussion. In the old days, he snapped his fingers and things happened.

He hates the way things are now. It is *so unfair*.

Eck tilts his head and gently licks Bob's ear with his long sticky tongue. It is his special way of expressing sympathy and it is not effective.

6

In the beginning, the earth was without form and void and the darkness was upon the face of the deep. And the spirit of God moved upon the face of the waters. And God said, 'Let there be light,' and there was light.

Only it wasn't very good light. Bob created fireworks, sparklers and neon tubes that circled the globe like weird tangled rainbows. He dabbled with bugs that blinked and abstract creatures whose heads lit up and cast long overlapping shadows. There were mile-high candles and mountains of fairy lights. For an hour or so, Earth was lit by enormous crystal chandeliers.

Bob thought his creations were very cool.

They *were* very cool, but they didn't work.

So Bob tried for an ambient glow (which proved toxic) and a blinding light in the centre of the planet, which gave off too much heat and fried the place black. And finally, when he curled up in the corner of the nothingness, tired as a child by the harebrainedness of his efforts, Mr B took the opportunity to sort things out – with an external star, gravity, roughly half the cycle in darkness and half in light so that there was a Day and a Night. And that was that. The evening and the morning were the first day. Not fancy, but it worked.

All of this happened while Bob napped. When he awoke, light was no longer an issue, and he'd mainly forgotten about it in any case. He'd moved on to waters and heavens, dry land and great oceans. Mr B hadn't ever seen anything like it, but he shrugged. Why not? Maybe the kid had some kind of a plan.

And Bob said, 'Let the earth bring forth grass and the fruit tree,' and it did, and Mr B had to admit that many of the fruits were inventive and delicious, with one or two exceptions – pomegranates, which seemed to be all form and no function, and lemons, which caused his mouth to purse up like a duck's anus and caused Bob to howl with laughter until he fell over into the oceans and had to scramble spluttering to safety.

Bob looked at all he'd done so far and saw that it was good. And he said, 'Let the waters bring forth abundant species of fish-like creatures, and fowl ones too.' And, boy oh boy, did Bob go to town on the creatures. He put spines on some, and strange colours on others; he added feathers and scales, and sometimes feathers *and* scales; and savage sharp teeth and beady eyes on some, and sweet expressions and razor-sharp claws on others. Some of the fowl were lovely to look at, with long graceful necks and luxuriant plumage, but others had the most idiotically large feet, or wings that didn't work.

Having neglected to create food for the carnivores, they began to eat one another almost immediately, which disturbed Mr B and didn't seem to be a temporary aberration but a situation destined to get far, far worse.

He began to suspect the boy was flying blind.

But before despair had a chance to take root, Bob suggested (with an annoying touch of noblesse oblige) that Mr B create something himself. Though reluctant at first, B began to picture a race of majestic sleek creatures with gently smiling faces and powerful tails that swept through the seas at wondrous speeds – yet breathed air and gave birth to live young. They lived underwater, but were not alien and cold-blooded like fish, and their voices were eloquent and haunting.

And so he created the great whales, which even Bob had to admit were pretty nice. And Mr B watched in awe as the blue-black waters magically parted for his creations and closed over them once they'd passed through. Long after Bob had moved on to create a whole slew of idiosyncratic aberrations (like platypus and slow lorises), Mr B stared with happy wonder at his whales.

'How beautiful you are,' he whispered to them, and they smiled back at him with their subtle smiles, happy to be admired.

And then Bob went on to create every creeping thing, and some that leapt and climbed and slithered and tunnelled as well, and he told them to be frantic and multiply, which they did by the most gobsmackingly weird mechanism Mr B had ever observed, one that slightly embarrassed him as well. He wanted to tap the boy on the shoulder and say, 'Excuse my presumption, but are you quite certain about that?'

In the meantime, Bob was jumping up and down and pronouncing it all 'good good good', *so* good that he couldn't stop giggling with self-satisfied glee like a demented toddler.

And then, like the child who couldn't resist adding more sprinkles to an already overloaded ice cream, he bestowed upon his creations a cacophony of different languages, so that they couldn't communicate with one another, and tied the weather to his moods just for fun, so that when he was cheerful the sun would shine, and when he was unhappy it would rain and storm and make everyone else unhappy too. When, eventually, B asked (with a great deal of respect he didn't feel) how it was all going to work *ensemble*, Bob didn't seem to understand the question, and Mr B sank deeper than before into gloom.

And then Bob blessed the whole misshapen weirdo lot of them, but not before performing an act of creation so audacious, so utterly appalling, so suicidal and wrong, that Mr B felt something must be done at once to stop him. He created man in *his own image*, and gave him dominion over the fish of the sea and the birds of the air, and the cattle and every creeping thing that creepeth upon the earth.

Which anyone could see was one big fat recipe for disaster.

And when, finally, on the sixth day, Bob sat back (like the smug know-nothing Mr B had become utterly convinced that he was) and said that it was very, *very* good, really amazingly good, adding that he'd like to have a rest now because all that creation had tired him out, B stared at him aghast and thought: You'd better get as much rest as you can, buddy boy, because you've just created one monster mess on your precious little planet and the minute all those hungry fish and fowl and idiot carnivores with spines and sharp teeth and tiny little brains get together there's going to be a bloodbath.

And as he thought those very words, the first lion ate the first antelope. And concluded that it was very good indeed.

The more Mr B thought about it the more anxious he became. Not only was he stuck with Bob himself, but with an entire race created in the image of that skinny arrogant dimwit. This was not Mr B's idea of a very good, or even a fair or a poor idea, or anything short of one more step on the road to eternal damnation.

Which is pretty much what it turned out to be.

7

'How lovely of you to phone, Lucy darling. Nothing's wrong?'

'You phoned me, Mother. And of course nothing's wrong.'

'Well, I won't keep you, but I did want to say that there's a wonderful sale on at –'

Lucy sighed. 'No thank you, Mother. I'm fine for clothes.'

'Of course you are.' She paused. 'And how's work?'

'All right, I guess. I'm supposed to hear if I've passed my three-month trial this week. I wish they'd tell me.' Tomorrow was Friday. How much longer would she have to wait? 'It's driving me mad.'

'Never mind, darling. I'm sure you've passed. You work so hard.'

Lucy grimaced. Her mother didn't know the first thing about office politics, and how difficult it was to keep a job these days. 'I'm going to be late if I don't get dressed.'

Mrs Davenport cleared her throat. 'You know, Althea's getting married at Christmas.'

Lucy said nothing.

'Aunt Evelyn phoned last night asking how many we'd be.'

'Let's see,' Lucy said tightly. 'Me, you and Dad. Let's call that three. Shall I count again?'

'No, of course not, darling, only, she said you could bring a date if you –'

'Goodbye, Mother.' The violence with which she banged the phone down caused the bedside lamp to sway dangerously. Reaching for it, Lucy knocked over her cup of tea. A warm brown stain spread across the white sheepskin rug by her bed.

'Oh, *shit*!' Lucy felt like crying. It was all her mother's fault.

Even if you hadn't actually met Lucy's mother, you might feel that you knew someone very like her. Laura Davenport had the air of an expensive pony – sturdy, alert and well-groomed. Sometime in the past, she had swapped her wanton youth for a prudent marriage and an attractive home in the Regency style, and now lived the life of a proper suburban wife. She specialized in expensive tweeds and cashmere cardigans in useful colours, cooked an excellent roast beef and only occasionally wondered how her life might have turned out differently.

None of these sensible qualities had quite prepared her for the emergence of her younger daughter, who resembled no one in the family, either in appearance or nature. Lucy was the sort of generous-breasted creamy-skinned hour-glass-figured young woman worshipped by artists and lovers from an earlier era, when words like Rubenesque expressed a pure admiration of rose-tinted faces poised serenely above monumental breasts, rippled thighs and dimpled buttocks; bodies that looked most alluring when dressed in nothing but a large gilt frame. With her small ankles and her pale gold hair, Lucy was a creature designed for an earlier sensibility, her shape unfashionable, perhaps, but gorgeous.

Like many girls her age, Lucy yearned for love. This should not have been difficult to realize. But the same luminosity that attracted perfect strangers also impeded her. Some men took her dramatic outline for evidence that she was stupid. Some assumed she must be arrogant. Others guessed that she'd never consider them anyway, so why make the effort? A surprising number of potential partners were thereby eliminated before she'd even had a chance to learn their names.

And then there was her mother, always nudging her in the direction of suitable men, while hinting that *in her day*, you didn't just sit around waiting for Mr Right; you went out, were proactive. The result of all this proactivity struck Lucy as equivocal. Her mother had obviously experienced many things in her time, but had ended up marrying her father – a perfectly dear man, but one with whom (even to Lucy's affectionate eye) she appeared to have little in common. Lucy's brain slid to her godfather, Bernard, as it had many times over the years. Had her mother been proactive with him?

Oh, to hell with everyone else, she thought. She was only twenty-one. There was plenty of time to sort out her love life. And anyway, it was hardly a tragedy to be a virgin at her age. No matter how much it felt like one.

Lucy scrambled for her keys, phone and bag, locked the door and ran to the bus stop – late and bad-tempered thanks to her mother and the spilled tea. Unless the bus came right away, she'd have no time to stop for breakfast. Nothing till eleven. The thought of which made her even grumpier.

But the bus came at once, traffic was light and the driver made six green lights in a row. By the time Lucy reached her stop she was feeling infinitely cheerier.

The café owner greeted her with a wave. 'Toast?'

'Two,' she said. 'And coffee, please.' What a difference it made just to see a friendly face in the morning. A bit of pleasant human contact was all it took to lift her mood, and by the time she reached work she was feeling cheerful again. After coffee and toast she began to wonder how she'd ever managed to feel out of sorts. Life's pleasures were so simple, really. It was all a matter of appreciating what you had – and knowing that things could be always be worse.

8

Bob's mother is playing poker and drinking gin. Having played a great number of winning hands, she concludes that the gin must be lucky and begins to order doubles. Hand after hand, the cards line up for her in flushes, straights and pairs, until Mona's pile of chips forms a large undulating wall behind which she can hide her delight.

Bob shows up late, as usual, accompanied by Eck. He takes the empty seat next to his mother and nods at the dealer. Eck moves at once to the edge of the table, eyeing a plate of sandwiches with naked lust.

'And who's this?' Mona coos delightedly in the direction of the little creature. 'What an adorable thing. Is he your . . .' She raises a suggestive eyebrow.

'My *what*?'

'Your child?' She wiggles her fingers, but the little beast keeps his distance, stretching his nose as far as it extends and sniffing cautiously in the direction of her hand.

'*My child?* Of course he's not my child. Look at him! He's an Eck, for God's sake. Is that my nose? Get a grip, Mother. He's nothing. Just a thing.'

A thing? The Eck frowns and puffs up his fur in outrage. He has always considered himself a step or two up from a thing.

'Come here, little Eck-thing,' Mona coaxes, and when the Eck takes a step closer, she pats his head, smooths down his soft fur and coos. 'Cute thing. Nice thing. Are you certain he's not yours, darling? There's something around the mouth that's just exactly reminiscent of you when you were a wee –'

Bob narrows his eyes and scowls.

Across from Mona, Mr Emoto Hed clears his throat. 'Are we here to gab or to gamble?' His voice contains a rumbling threat. Despite a soft spot for Mona, he has no affection for her son, who has a habit of hanging around at card games helping himself to his mother's winnings.

Even when he likes people, Mr Hed is not one for making himself pleasant.

Next to Hed sits his daughter, Estelle, a somewhat self-effacing girl with quiet manners and a cool intellect. She never gambles. Now she looks at Eck. 'Hello,' she says. 'What a lovely creature.'

'*Love-ly?*' Bob pokes Eck in the ribs, toppling him. He yelps in pain. 'Hear that? She thinks you're *lovely.*'

Estelle, who has clocked the direction of Eck's yearning, picks up the large plate of sandwiches and offers them. Eck's eyes are huge with longing. He devours the lot in less time than it takes to blink and then slumps, sedated, against his benefactor's leg. She reaches down to stroke him and he purrs sleepily.

Another hand is dealt and Mona picks hers up slowly. Nothing. She folds.

Bob frowns and follows, slapping his cards down on the table with peevish force. The noise makes Eck jump.

Her next hand is so spectacularly bad that Mona begins to suspect foul play, flicking her eyes (a little unsteadily) from one neutral face to the next. She draws three cards and calls for another gin.

By the twenty-fourth worst hand in the history of poker, Mona's fortune has diminished to a pile of chips the size of a teacup. She casts about, scrutinizing her opponents. Of course, each has the capacity – that is to say, the *power* – to cheat, but galactic poker is inviolate, and no one in the long and tangled history of the game has ever cheated. Or at least admitted to cheating.

For the next hand, the dealer flips her a two of spades, a four of clubs, one joker, a picture of a furry kitten and a postcard from Marbella.

Mona leaps up in a fury and staggers, nearly tipping the table. All at once she is thirty feet tall. Flames shoot from the tips of her fingers and lap round her giant torso. Her bronze and copper hair snakes in wild flaming tendrils round her head. 'Someone is *asss*-tempting to *imp*-fluence this game,' she says in her best steel-dipped-in-gin purr. 'And when I find out who it is the consequences will be . . . calum-nitudinal. Catastropherous.' She sways, the gin swooshing catastropherously behind her eyes.

'Sit down, Mother,' hisses Bob.

Mr Hed smiles, and Estelle looks down at her hands. Every other player concentrates on his or her own expression of shocked innocence. 'I am greatly hurt by your accusation,' says Emoto Hed mildly, rising slowly to his feet in a great crackling magnetic disturbance. Slowly, in mirror motion, he and Mona sit down.

The game continues.

9

Mr B stares at the huge stack of paperwork, hands laid softly on the fine ebonized surface of his Biedermeier secretaire, in readiness, like a pianist about to launch into Liszt. He absently traces a pale maple flicker in the wood before choosing a file and removing it from the heap. With a sense of deep dejection he opens it. He remembers purchasing this desk in Vienna, sometime after Napoleon's armies were dealt their final blow at Waterloo. It might have been only last week, so recent does it seem.

He tries not to dwell on the past. No point, he tells himself. This is how he has survived thus far, one foot in front of the other, nice and steady. And if his dedication has shown any sign of flagging, it is only the hopeless, the relentless, the unworthy stupidity of the colossal idiotic . . .

Stop. Stop.

He drops his head into his hands.

At last he pulls out a file, *the* file, the all-important file, his letter of resignation. He has checked and rechecked every word, every line, dotted every 'i', crossed every 't'. Now, at last, he is ready. He is utterly certain of its perfection, and of his need to submit it at once. The time is right. Holding his breath (for this is a moment of great solemnity, the gentle nudging of the first domino in what he hopes will become a long series of follow-on actions), he slides the letter into an envelope with exquisite care, seals it and . . . there. It is gone.

A deep breath. The die is cast. Surely the committee will take pity, or, if not pity, will at least recognize the desperation, the logical argument he has made for a long rest, or a different sort of job (more menial if need be, though preferably – in recognition of excellence over time – a superior desk job somewhere). As long as it's stress-free. Quiet. No Bob.

He savours the moment with something between elation and fear. Change is possible after all. He exalts in the step he has managed to take at last. Six weeks' notice, and then the future beckons with its vast postbag of possibilities. He will concentrate on his exit strategy. Not long now. Plenty to do in preparation. He lets his breath out with a sigh.

If he were a different sort of man, he would scream, sing, leap with joy.

He pushes his spectacles back up to the bridge of his nose. Now that the thing is done, there's the day's work to be getting on with. Mr B eyes the untidy heaps of prayers, his heart filled with the knowledge that this process is finite, at least as far as he is concerned. W today. War (genocide/massacres/ethnic cleansing), Water (polluted/lack of/poisoned), Widows and Wills (unfair/illegally altered). He singles out the file marked Whales.

Every day he thinks of his whales. When his patience for Bob wanes to its lowest ebb, he thinks of them, big and solemn, with their deep echoing songs. They are his. Of course Bob's work is not without things to admire. Mr B marvels that the same God who leaves his dirty clothes in a mouldering heap by the side of his bed could have created golden eagles and elephants and butterflies. Such moments of transcendent inspiration! Other creatures fill him with admiration as well – heavy loping striped tigers and graceful long-necked swans, creaking as they fly. Ludicrous pincush-ion porcupines. It's not that the boy is altogether devoid of talent, but he is devoid of discipline, compassion and emotional depth. Foresight.

How is it, he wonders, that Bob has managed to remain so detached from his more beautiful creations? It's his atten-tion span as much as anything, his inability to sustain interest, the tendency to discard his new toys in some barren corner of the Earth where they gather dust while he pursues (yet another) hotted-up floozy.

Mr B looks out of the window. Had the job seemed such a bad idea at the time? 'We need you,' they'd said, 'your experience, your stability, your people skills.' No description, conveniently, of the loser they'd appointed with him.

Let's face it, he'd been flattered. They'd known exactly what sugared words to whisper in his ear as they lowered the noose.

'Impossible job to fill,' they'd told him. And they'd known. Oh yes, he was certain now that they'd known from the beginning. The boy was obviously thick as a divot, and if there hadn't been a push from someone with a bit of influ-ence he'd still be out in the middle of the great galactic nothingness, sleeping, probably, or picking his nose.

'He'll grow into the job,' they'd assured him, 'gain stature along the way.' Of course he hadn't, and in the end, no one cared. There were so many more advanced corners of the universe requiring attention.

Mr B sighs.

At least Bob has gone out. Let him be someone else's problem tonight.

10

The dealer deals.

Mona's cards, a full house of aces and kings, makes her think that perhaps she's been a bit hasty in accusing Hed of cheating. Perhaps she's just been unlucky. Ha ha, she thinks, and pushes what is left of her chips into the centre of the table.

Hed lays down a royal flush.

The players leap up as one. Mona bursts into flame, and when Hed offers the next bet at double or nothing she accepts immediately, some might say precipitously. Never a player to quit while the going is good, Mona casts about for a stake.

Bob looks bored.

'Well?' says Hed. Menace rises from him like dust.

Mona's eyes come to rest on the Eck. With a quick lunge, she grabs him round the middle and sets him on to the table, where he stands, blinking.

'Here,' says Mona.

'What kind of a stake is that?' Hed's face registers disdain.

Bob yawns, pushes the hair out of his eyes. 'He's the last of the Ecks. After him, they're extinct.'

'Very valuable,' says Mona eagerly.

Trembling, the Eck seeks sympathy from one impassive face after another.

'Just one left. Rarer than rare.' Mona's eyes glitter unnaturally.

Estelle stands up. 'Stop,' she says quietly. And then louder, '*Stop!*'

Everyone turns to look at her.

'Put him back on the floor. He is a creature, not a thing.'

'He's *mine*,' insists Mona, 'and I can do with him what I like.' To prove her point, she pokes him. He gives a little cry and Mona turns to Hed. 'That's my stake. The last of the Ecks. His life. To do with what you will.'

Estelle turns to one of the other players. 'Make some black coffee, please.' She looks back at Mona, who is waving her glass over her head for a refill, and puts one hand out to stop the waiter from stepping forward. 'That's enough, Mona.' Her voice is calm. 'Eck, you can go.'

'No he can't,' Mona says firmly. 'He's *my* Eck.' Her eyes lock Hed's, glinting.

'He's *my* Eck, actually,' Bob mutters. 'You never even noticed him before today.'

Hed sneers. 'What would I want with him anyway? So he's the last of the Ecks. He's still worthless.'

The little creature droops.

Mona leans in, a bit loopy with gin, and lowers her voice. 'Ecks are said to have the sweetest-tasting meat of any creature in nine thousand galaxies.' She holds Hed's gaze and lowers her voice still further to a whisper. 'Just between you and me, that's why he's the last one.'

Bob rolls his eyes.

This proves too much for the Eck, who squeaks with outrage and crumples into himself. Estelle reaches out to him. 'No one,' she says quietly, 'is going to eat you.' She turns to her father. 'Are you?'

Neither Mona nor Hed will show weakness by being the first to look away. 'The sweetest meat in nine thousand galaxies?' Hed looks thoughtful. 'How is it that I have never tasted Eck?' He thinks for a moment and then holds out his hand. 'Done. I accept your stake.'

'Just a minute. He's my Eck, not yours.' Bob's glare takes in his mother and Hed. 'If anyone's going to eat him, it should be me.'

Estelle lifts the Eck off the table. 'Don't listen,' she whispers. To the assembled players, she speaks sternly. 'Stop this now. It isn't right. You know it isn't right. Bob? He's your pet. Don't let them do this.'

Bob slumps deep in his chair. 'Let's get on with the game. I've got stuff to do.'

Smiling grimly, Mona produces a brand-new deck of cards and hands it to the dealer, who unwraps it and deals. The game is over in less than a minute.

When he realizes what has happened, the Eck begins to wail.

Mona retires unsteadily, her eyes crossed. Bob follows, muttering. The players disperse.

Estelle places one firm hand on her father's arm. 'Daddy, you can't eat him.'

'A bet is a bet.'

'Only if you say it is,' says Estelle.

36

Emoto Hed smiles his not very nice smile. 'I'm quite looking forward to my first taste of Eck. And my last, obviously.' He laughs a not very nice laugh.

The Eck shrinks.

'Not in front of him, please, Daddy.'

Hed drums his fingers. 'I won the Eck fair and square and he's mine to eat if I want to.'

'I won't let him be eaten.' Estelle's face is composed and just the slightest bit stern. Her voice is cool.

Hed's eyes darken. Black smoke rolls off him in stinking waves. 'A deal,' he rumbles in a voice deep as death, 'is a deal.'

Estelle does not flinch.

Her father's presence becomes a devastating absence, a malignant Hed-shaped void sucking all light and heat into its core.

But his daughter is unfazed. Everywhere Hed looks he meets her gaze. At last he sighs, ceases to smoke, becomes manifest once more. 'Only, you know what an old softie I am. He can have a reprieve.'

Estelle lets her guard down a fraction. Her eyes soften and she places her hand on his arm. 'Thank you, Daddy. I knew you'd see sense.'

'Six weeks. And then I eat him.'

She stiffens. 'Six weeks?'

'Six weeks. It'll give him time to get used to the idea.'

Eck scrambles to the floor and over to the furthest corner of the room, where he slumps like a half-deflated football. He does not think he will get used to the idea.

Quietly, so as not to offend, he begins to cry.

11

Mona slept like a child, a drunken child, her pale brow flushed, her arms flung out across the bed in abandon. Bob paced, desperate to leave, but not before a much-needed confrontation with his mother.

He sat down on the bed and shoved her.

Mona groaned; the lovely features crumpled in pain. 'Ohhh, ouch.' Her right hand drifted up from her side, settling on one soft cheek. She pressed her slender fingers gently against a throbbing cheekbone. 'Oh, Bob, my darling. It's you.'

'Yes, it's me, Mother. Me. *Alone*. Minus something, Mother.' He glared.

'You should never let me drink so much,' she said, with a brave attempt at a smile.

'Oh, ha. Like I could have stopped you.'

She groaned gently. 'A big handsome boy like you.' The words emerged slightly slurred, as if the act of speaking caused her pain. 'Against poor little me.'

'Poor little you?' Bob snorted. 'Look, I'm going now. But I want to know what you plan to do about my Eck.'

'Your Eck?'

Bob rolled his eyes. 'Don't you remember anything about last night?'

She hazarded a guess. 'Did I lose?'

'Duh.'

'Badly?'

'DUH.'

'Oh, well.' She closed her eyes again. 'What shall we do today? I'll feel better in a minute.'

'*Mother.*'

'Yes, darling?'

'You stole my pet.'

Her eyes fluttered open. 'Did I? Silly old me.'

Bob's eyes flashed fire. 'You stole my Eck and he's going to be *eaten.*'

'Don't tell me now, darling. It's too early. I haven't the strength.'

'It's noon, actually, and I want him back.'

Mona sighed. 'I'll get you another one, my darling. Ecks are always around, cheap as chips. Get under your feet like dustballs.' She frowned. 'Or at least they used to. Back before the crazy rumour about them tasting absolutely amazing.' She laughed weakly. 'Luckily, Hed knows nothing about that.'

Bob groaned.

Mona's eyes opened wide in horror. 'Hed *knows*? Who could possibly have been so indiscre–'

The expression on her son's face stopped her.

'Oh.'

'According to what *you* told the assembled company, Mother, he's not only the last of the Ecks, but the most delicious-tasting dish in nine thousand galaxies.'

'That doesn't seem right.' Mona appeared genuinely puzzled, though whether by the morality of the situation or the slightly suspect nature of the story, was unclear.

Bob leapt to his feet and began to pace. 'This is just the sort of thing you always do.'

'Always?' Mona frowned. 'Have I gambled away Ecks before?'

He stopped. Swivelled to face her. 'I want him back. I'm sick of you stealing my things.' His voice rose to a shout. 'GET HIM BACK.'

'Yes, darling. What a good plan. I'll do that. In a minute.' If only her son would make less of a racket. Or, better yet, disappear altogether. Never mind. She would wear something nice and go to see Hed and he would give her back the Eck. Of course he would.

In the meantime, breakfast might help the pounding pain behind her eyes. She would sort out the bet. But only when her head had stopped hurting. When Bob had stopped shouting at her. When she was feeling herself once more.

Perhaps not even then. But definitely not before.

12

Estelle took the long way back to Bob's, carrying the Eck in her arms. The creature weighed roughly the same as a year-old child and felt similarly heavy and compact, like a dumpling. He settled into her arms with a sigh, his nose curled gently round the back of her neck.

They stopped at a café, where Estelle ordered four poached eggs with bacon, sausage, beans and extra buttered toast, plus a side order of crispy waffles with butter, powdered sugar and syrup, three chocolate muffins and a bowl of hot milk. She cut the waffles and sausage into small pieces, and watched with amusement as the Eck attempted to stuff an entire chocolate muffin into his (already quite full) mouth.

It wasn't till he had finished the last crumb of waffle and drunk the last drop of milk that the Eck's eyes began to close and he slumped down on Estelle's lap.

The only other customer was a pretty blonde girl, who smiled at Estelle. Estelle smiled back.

'Oh my heavens,' said the girl, her eyes wide with wonder. 'What sort of creature is *that*?'

'He's from Madagascar,' Estelle said. 'And is somewhat rare.'

'*Very* rare, I'd say. I've never seen anything like him. And so tame! May I pet him?'

Estelle nodded, and the girl giggled as she stroked Eck's long flexible nose. 'I work at the zoo,' she said, pointing in the direction of the blue hippo pools on the side of the hill. 'And we don't have anything remotely like him. Has he got a name?'

'He's an Eck,' Estelle said, and Lucy later wished she'd asked the girl how to spell it, for she was unable to find reference to an Eck or an Ecc or an Ech or an Ecqu on the website of Malagasy fauna.

Estelle waited till Lucy had gone, paid the bill and scooped the bulging Eck up in her arms once more. Together they strolled in the glorious morning sun, the sleepy creature rousing himself now and again to stare over Estelle's shoulder. Bob never took him for walks.

Estelle talked to him as they strolled, not always about things he understood. But her voice seemed to enclose him in a warm place full of light, and he felt safe.

When she could no longer put off the inevitable, she made her way to Bob's flat and stood in the doorway, the creature in her arms, reluctant to give him up. The expression on her face was grave. 'My father has given him a reprieve,' she told Bob. 'A short one, unfortunately. Those of us with an interest will naturally involve ourselves in helping him. I trust you will treat him well in the meantime.'

'Eck,' sighed Eck, his thoughts straying to sticky waffles and jam.

Bob glanced at Estelle with no sign of recognition, then

at his pet. 'Well, it's about time you made it home. Who's the girl? Bring me my toast. I'm starving.'

Estelle tilted her head and looked carefully at Bob.

Bob huffed. '*What?*'

Estelle placed Eck on the floor and adjusted his sweater. 'I'll be back,' she said to his enquiring look. And left.

'So . . . a temporary reprieve, eh? Great. When you're done with the toast, tell B that I need him.' Bob poked Eck in the solar plexus with a pencil. The creature squeaked and trotted off with a wounded expression.

He returned in seconds. 'Eck,' he said.

Bob glowered. 'You didn't even ask him. Where's my toast?'

'Eck!'

'You ate it, didn't you?'

Eck jumped up and down in protest. 'Eck! Eck! Eck!'

Bob caught hold of Eck's prehensile nose and pulled him close. 'You're bad.'

Eck stood his ground, glaring. You're bad too.

'I'm not bad. I'm *God*.'

Bad God, thought Eck. Rubbish crap horrid God.

They stared at each other, hostile and unblinking, until at last Bob tired of the stand-off, picked Eck up and flung him into a wicker basket, wedged it under the bed and flounced off to find Mr B. Eck wept with rage, holding his tender nose.

'I need to talk to you.'

The older man did not look up from his work. 'Talk away.'

'I need your full attention.'

'Of course.' More easily said than done. Listening to Bob

43

was like watching a particularly enervating version of reality TV; one could engage fully only when armed with a good book, a drink and a head full of tertiary thoughts. Mr B arranged his features in a manner likely to express interest. 'Shoot,' he said genially.

'I'm going out now.'

'Righty-ho.'

'Don't you want to know where?'

'Of course.' Not. But he knew, without having to be told. A few millennia were more than enough to get inside the head of a self-important twank motivated exclusively by food, sex and the avoidance of pain.

Bob set his shoulders. 'I am going to see Lucy.' He paused, struck a pose and gazed towards the window, affecting indifference. A loud shuffling noise from Bob's bedroom heralded the reappearance of Eck, who positioned himself on the mantel behind Bob and mimicked the boy's sullen slouch precisely. Mr B stifled a laugh.

'Excellent. Send her my love. Use a condom. Try not to talk about your job too much – you know the effect it has on women.'

Bob frowned. 'Aren't you even going to . . .'

'No.'

The boy's frown deepened, his entire body forming a pout. Behind him, Eck adopted the stance in miniature, his face a perfect caricature of Bob's.

'Right, then. I'm off.' He didn't budge.

Mr B slid his spectacles back over his eyes and returned to work, waiting for the sound of footsteps.

None came.

The two held this pose as Mr B's watch ticked off the seconds. 'I thought you were going,' he said at last.

One fat tear ran down the boy's smooth cheek, the eternally fair cheek eternally uncreased with anxiety, despite the eternally God-awful facts of his existence.

'Off you go, then. I've work to do. I always have work to do, in case you hadn't noticed – moving my infinite mountain of sand with my infinitely small tweezers.'

Eck looked from one face to the other. He sidled sideways towards Mr B, choosing sides.

Bob's face crumpled. 'I need help.'

'Yes, indeed, matey, I need help too. I've got poisonous floods in one half of the world and crippling drought in the other. I thought you were going to sort out some of the wetness issues. Did you even read the notes I gave you? It wasn't difficult. Africa: wet. America: dry.'

'I did what you said.' God's outraged voice flew up an octave.

Hands on hips, Eck embodied disbelief.

'Did you? Did you really? Because, you see, I'm thinking that there's just the faintest of chances that you got it backwards. Maybe, just *maybe*, you weren't quite paying attention when I explained the situation to you with such care, so that you muddled your landmasses? Is that remotely possible?' Mr B paused and removed his spectacles, revealing eyes glittering with barely contained fury. 'Let me tell you why I'm asking. I'm asking because I've got four million people displaced by flood in Florida and five million dying of thirst in the Sudan. It's just a guess, a wild guess, but I'm thinking *just possibly* you mixed the two up.'

45

The boy looked away, his face holy with pain. 'It wasn't my fault. Your writing's so hard to read. And you *know* how I mix up my letters. Bad/dab/pad/bod. It's that disease. Dyspepsia.'

Mr B sighs. 'Not bad/bod. *Not* pad/pod. A-mer-i-ca. Af-ri-ca. This time I thought I explained the difference so that even *you* might remember. But you weren't listening, were you?' He pressed a hand to his forehead, hard, as if to contain the wrath within.

God rolled his eyes. 'Sor-*ry*,' he drawled.

Mr B breathed deeply, drumming his fingers on the pale maple. 'You see, you see, let me explain. *Sorry*, as a word, as a concept, used properly in this context, suggests contrition, regret, remorse. And, oddly enough, remorse is *not* what's communicating itself to me. I'm not *actually* getting a sense that you give a rat's arse whether the whole bloody world goes to hell in a hand basket while you pursue congress with this week's Zeppelin-titted trollop.'

The truth of this could not be denied. Bob had created the world and then simply lost interest. Since his second week of employment, he'd passed the time sleeping and playing with his wangle, while managing to ignore the existence of his creations entirely.

And was this an excuse for him to be rained with curses and loathing from all mankind? Oh no. Because here was the clever bit: *Bob had designed the entire race of murderers, martyrs and thugs with a built-in propensity to worship him.* You had to admire the kid. Thick as two lemons, but with flashes of brilliance so intense a person could go blind looking at him.

The older man replaced his spectacles and looked carefully at his charge. For whole moments at a time, you could almost feel sorry for him. He did look lost. And if (by some quirk of fate) Mr B happened to be in the mood to notice, he could see the isolation that enveloped Bob like a shroud, and the sadness too.

Well, it was his own damned fault. No one forced him to take a job for which he was singularly unqualified. No one forced him to create such a mess. And if his only friend was that execrable penguiny *thing*, whose fault was that? Not mine, thought Mr B.

The boy squirmed, long skinny legs wrapped round each other, rib-cage twisted ninety degrees from his hips in what appeared to be an impossible configuration of limbs. His elbows jutted out abruptly from his sides like some sort of drafting error and (independently aware of their awkwardness) his arms wound themselves round his torso like vines. Eck straddled his shoulder, alert for the swat of a hand. When it came, he ducked.

'I. Need. Help.' Lord, he hated asking for it. 'With Lucy.'

And Lord, how Mr B hated to give it. 'Can't you just do the usual? Appear to her in a vision, give her a stigmata or two, blacken up your eyes, assume your most mournful expression? Don't they always fall for the hollow-eyed holy-seer thing?' Mr B recognized the cycle: unrequited lust, idealized passion, consummation . . . and then he'd be on to the next, leaving the latest victim seduced, ruined and abandoned. What was wrong with him that (in how many dozens of millennia?) he'd never managed to learn anything useful from experience?

'I can't. Because . . .' His voice was hoarse.

Because she's perfect. You should see her, so beautiful . . .

'Because she's perfect,' Bob sighed. 'You should see her, so beautiful and clever —'

And kind!

'— and kind. This time I think . . .'

She could really be the one.

'. . . she could really be the one.'

Well, perhaps I'm predictable too, thought Mr B. They'd had a very long time to get to know each other. A very long time.

Bob narrowed his eyes. 'Are you going to help me or not?'

'Not.'

'Well, then.' The boy assumed a self-righteous air. 'I feel it only fair to warn you that whatever happens between Lucy and myself, whatever — as you put it — *congress* occurs, will be none of your business. So don't come round later asking me what happened, or blaming me, because, as of this minute, I am not telling you anything about my life, *ever again*.' Bob dematerialized into a pillar of molten silver and disappeared with a deafening crash. Eck scurried after him.

Mr B sighed. Thank heavens for a bit of peace and quiet. And if he never tells me anything about his life ever again, I'll rejoice for a million and twelve years.

13

Luke's PA waved and told her to go in.

Lucy knocked on his office door, softly at first, her heart thumping. It was just her luck to be called into *his* office, to get the verdict from *him*. But he couldn't dislike her enough to deny her the job. Could he? Even Luke wouldn't be so mean.

Receiving no response, she took a deep breath and tried again, with more force. Maybe he wasn't in after all. She bent closer to listen, her ear nearly touching the door, when it swung open abruptly, unbalancing her so that she stumbled and caught Luke hard in the chest with one elbow.

'Ouch.' He stared at her.

Lucy blushed. Why did this sort of thing always happen around him? 'I was just . . . you didn't answer.'

'Come in.' His voice was cool.

She sat down at the edge of a metal folding chair. It was warm in the office; sun streamed through a window propped open with a book. The air coming in from outside smelled of lilac and new grass.

Luke stared down at the paperwork on his desk, no

happier with this arrangement than she was. Why was it incumbent upon him to give her the news? He'd held out as long as possible, hoping for an excuse to reverse the decision. At last he shoved a folder at her across his desk. 'There,' he said, looking beyond her to the wall behind.

She picked up the papers and quickly leafed through. Contract of employment, permanent ID card. Yes!

'Congratulations.' His tone was flat. 'Any questions?'

Lord almighty, she thought, what is wrong with him? 'No, no questions. Thank you. I mean, I'm really happy. This is great.' She got up to leave but hovered an instant too long. 'I love my job, you know,' she said with dignity. 'And I'm grateful to have passed my trial.'

He said nothing.

With as much grace as she could muster, Lucy turned and left his office. Sweat trickled down the small of her back. Her knees felt weak.

Mica smiled at her as she shut the door. 'Well done. Now you're stuck here.'

'Thank you. What a relief.'

'You don't look happy enough.'

She rolled her eyes. 'I always feel like such a geek around him. And a fraud. He makes me feel as if I don't deserve the job.'

'Ignore him, sweetheart. The guy was born cranky. Some girlfriend left him a million years ago and he's been hissy ever since. You probably remind him of her.'

'Yeah, that would explain it.' She sighed.

The office door opened again and Luke strode out,

dumping an armful of files on Mica's desk. 'I'm off,' he said with a wave to his PA, and was through the door before either had a chance to reply.

Lucy felt furious. He was perfectly capable of acting normal, though not, apparently, to her. She slumped down in the chair next to Mica. 'Why is he so horrible?'

Mica shrugged. 'Some guys just are. I'd have him, though.'

Lucy snorted. 'You're much too nice for him. Can't you find some sweet boy who'll cook and clean and be the perfect wife?'

'Nope. Big shoulders, square jaw, that's what I want. Preferably straight.'

'You're an idiot, Mica. It'll end in tears.'

'I know.' He sighed. 'But I'll have had fun trying.'

'Well, you can have him. Maybe he hates all women. That would make me feel better.'

'Me too, honey.'

Lucy went back to work, cheered. She loved her job. She loved the animals, loved the pygmy goats, wallabies and Komodo dragons, the African spiders, penguins, dung beetles and giant crickets. She loved walking the llamas round the perimeter of the zoo, loved doling out protein pellets and parrot seed and grass for the hippos. She couldn't think of any job that would make her feel happier or more fulfilled. And if staying on meant avoiding Luke, well then, she would simply avoid him.

Bob and Eck entered the zoo via the visitor's entrance, passing through the turnstile unnoticed. Taking a map from the volunteer at the information booth, Bob turned it over a dozen times before heading off in the wrong direction. He was beginning to grow steamy with frustration and anxiety, silently appealing to Mr B for help while Eck hid under a thorny hedge, peering, a bit nervously, at the animals in cages. As Bob consulted the map again, a tall ruminant with deep brown eyes, pursed lips and a thick mass of golden blond fur nearly ran him down.

'Excuse me,' gasped the keeper, hauling on a red lead rope and bringing the llama to a skidding stop. 'We didn't mean to run you over.' The llama sneered at Bob, but the girl smiled a smile like the light at the end of a tunnel. 'Are you all right?'

Bob smiled back and Lucy experienced a peculiar sensation of weightlessness, as if gravity had momentarily abandoned her. She blinked. He was gorgeous. Dazzlingly, astonishingly, gorgeous. He glowed, as if lit from within.

'I-I really am terribly sorry. This is Izzy – a Peruvian Ccara llama.'

'I'm Bob.' Bob's eyes blazed. Lucy! In the flesh! Her gaze was sweet and full of warmth, her eyes an extraordinary cerulean blue. The temperature rose ten degrees throughout the zoo and tulip buds burst open with little muted pops, spreading instantly into full flower.

My beautiful, beautiful Lucy, he thought.

'Izzy, meet Bob. Would you like to walk my llama, Bob?' She offered him the lead, unable to look at him full-on, her hand trembling a little. 'Usually it's a treat reserved for children, but –' she cast about quickly for Luke – 'we haven't got any school groups this morning. Go on, you'll like it. Izzy's special.'

Bob took the lead from her, his eyes riveted to the pale damp skin of her forearm. He felt an almost overwhelming desire to bend down and kiss it, but ran his hand down the llama's neck instead, burrowing his fingers deep into the soft gold of its fleece. His eyes half-closed in rapture. 'She's so soft,' he murmured.

'He. Izzy's short for Isambard. Look there.' She pointed to his undercarriage and there, indeed, was a large swinging pair of boy-llama testicles. 'His fur's lovely, isn't it?' She laughed.

Bob swallowed hard, unable to tear his eyes off the girl of his dreams. You beauty, he thought. I've searched the world for a girl like you. Dreamt about you. I love you. I love you more than any other woman on the entire planet. There is no other as lovely as you.

All at once, the llama, which had been walking quietly, began to dance and toss his head in an attempt to slip his collar. Izzy sensed something amiss with the person leading him; he had no experience of such a creature, and what he perceived made him anxious.

Lucy, meanwhile, considered Bob, more boldly now. He looked as familiar as a brother or . . . the prime minister. But how? She was certain she didn't know him. And yet, *she knew him.*

Their eyes met. Bob smiled and Lucy found herself flattened, shaken to the core. The smile was big and deep and soft, a smile that seemed to encompass a thousand extra dimensions of friendliness – with longing, affection, incipient love, and multiple human lifetimes of anticipation thrown in.

Behind them, sheet lightning ripped across the cloudless sky.

No one had ever smiled such a smile at Lucy before, but it seemed to be the smile she had waited her entire life to receive. She smiled back. Eck tilted his head sideways from under his thorny hedge and wondered if he owed her the courtesy of a warning. He was loyal to his master up to a point, but she looked just the sort of girl to walk straight into a crocodile's smiling jaws.

'Oh, Lucy, Lucy,' Bob murmured, elbowing the stroppy llama aside. But Izzy took umbrage. He orgled: a braying sort of cry. He didn't like Bob's smell and he didn't like being elbowed, particularly by someone whose smell he didn't like. Orgling again, louder and more aggressively this time, he drew his head back to spit.

Lucy wasn't precisely clear about what happened next, but Izzy seemed to flicker and fizz, like the badly focused picture on an old-fashioned television set. The noise he made was strangled; he sat back on his hocks, eyes wild and bulging. By the time Lucy had gained control of him and turned back to speak to her new acquaintance, Bob was gone.

How weird, she thought, him disappearing like that. Maybe he's here with his girlfriend? A guy like that must have a girlfriend. But what would they be doing here, on Friday morning, at the zoo? It was all so mysterious. Lucy could have wept with disappointment. 'Never mind, Izz,' she said sadly. 'Plenty of other fish in the sea.'

A few minutes later she stopped in her tracks and frowned. How on earth did he know my name?

Behind her, twenty-eight rainbows spread silently across the sky like oil in a puddle.

14

'Come in, Mona,' said Hed, patting the chair beside him. In a dress made from a book of twelve first-class stamps, Mona looked quite ravishing. She was a good-looking woman, Hed thought. Shame about the goofy son.

'You know why I'm here, of course?' She struggled to maintain her smile.

Hed shrugged and shook his head. 'Not a clue.' He sat back, linked his hands behind his head and began to whistle.

Mona shifted. 'It's Bob's pet. You see, it wasn't really a proper wager, because, strictly speaking, the Eck didn't belong to me.'

Hed's face showed no expression. 'I'm afraid I'm going to have to file that under Very Much Your Problem Not Mine.' His fathomless blank eyes narrowed. 'A bet is a bet, Mona. And I am greatly looking forward to tasting the most delicious creature in nine thousand galaxies.'

'Oh, that!' Mona tossed her head with nervous gaity. 'Ha ha ha ha! I was only repeating something I'd heard. You know what rumours are like, idle gossip, hardly ever any truth in them at all.'

A noise emerged from Hed's throat; it increased in volume,

like an avalanche. His features twisted; his words exploded in the air around her; he was everywhere and nowhere at once, inside of her and out. 'I sincerely hope, for your sake,' he thundered, 'that it turns out *not* to be a rumour.'

Mona gasped.

'Or I might find myself something else to devour.' The last words disappeared in a wall of sound.

She dragged herself away, struggling through the roar, her limbs heavy and dead, the noise swallowing her whole, digesting her.

'How'd it go?' Bob was waiting for her at home.

'Wonderfully well, darling, marvellously.' Mona smiled palely.

Bob glowered. 'You're lying.'

She held one hand to her forehead. 'Of course I'm not, sweetheart.'

'I don't believe you. But I suppose we'll know soon enough.'

Mona's expression turned furtive. 'Bob, darling.'

'Yes?'

'You wouldn't like to do me an itsy-bitsy little favour, would you?'

'No.'

She sighed. 'It's only that, well, I'd happily get you ten new pets if you'd just agree to forget this one.'

Bob stamped his foot. 'No! You never think about my feelings. Gambling away my pet is just *so typical*. You always do exactly what you like, barging in, grabbing up my stuff, throwing my Eck away in some *poxy* poker game without a thought for *me*. Well, I *don't* want ten other pets, I want *mine* . . .'

Mona wasn't listening. Of course a bet was a bet, she thought. And there was her reputation to consider. Not to mention her safety. Particularly her safety. For she was frightened of Emoto Hed, who had something of a reputation for creative cruelty where unpaid debts were concerned. People disappeared, leaving behind nothing but very long, very piercing screams. Mona imagined that forever could become incredibly tedious when passed in a state of constantly accelerating agony.

And, really. How much did an Eck matter anyway? Hardly at all, as far as Bob was concerned. She, herself, felt that the extinction of the Ecks would sadden no one but other Ecks, of which there would be none. Problem solved!

Perhaps the time for self-recrimination was past. If Hed wanted the last of the Ecks as a meal, she supposed it was his prerogative.

Bob's voice had risen to a scream. 'Like NOW! You're not even listening to me! What kind of mother do you call yourself?'

Mona just hoped Bob's pet didn't turn out to be stringy and bitter. It would be just her luck if this particular Eck ended up having the worst-tasting flesh in nine thousand galaxies.

She looked up. 'Sorry, darling, you were saying something?'

Bob's response could not be transcribed.

15

Lucy couldn't stop thinking about Bob. He wasn't a bit like anyone she'd met before. Not that she had a type, but, if she had one, Bob definitely wasn't it – too young, too awkward, too skinny. And yet . . . those deep-set eyes. The beautiful face. The strange intensity. The smile. And even more than all that – the inexplicable density of him, as if he were somehow *connected* to everything: past and present, earth and sky, life and death. She frowned. How to explain the strangeness of him, her sense of knowing him without really knowing?

Her last boyfriend had worked for a software company and, really, she'd barely known him at all. They'd had some fun, gone to a few films, sat up late listening to music – but he'd never seemed terribly interested in who she was and how she might be different from everyone else. He'd listened politely when she talked, but the questions he asked were never the right questions. Sometimes she felt like shouting at him, demanding to know why he never said the right thing. Not that it was his fault, exactly. If she were perfectly honest, she didn't find many of his thoughts terribly interesting either, and when the conversation stopped she'd had to scramble for something to say.

But Bob? This was different. After only a few minutes together, she'd experienced a sort of a buzz in her blood, a feeling of connection and at the same time exposure. What did she know about him? Exactly nothing. For all she knew, he could be crazy or a criminal or worse. *And how had he known her name?*

She thought about him as she fed and watered Isambard and moved on to the capybaras. They looked up as she entered their enclosure. Her favourite, a young male about the size of a sheep, trotted over and pressed his large blunt nose against her thigh.

'Hello, big boy,' she said, stroking the stiff coat. The raked half-closed eyes were sensual with drowsiness. Leaning almost all of his weight against her now, the gigantic rodent growled. 'Get off,' she said. 'I'll fetch some hay.'

Lucy pushed him and the animal teetered a few steps on incongruously slender legs. As she turned to go, the capy trotted after her, whining and pawing as she hauled half a bale of hay down into the enclosure and shook out the sections in a heap. Three non-dominant boars lay together in the outdoor mud pool, noses and ears sticking out as they wallowed, half-asleep, their backs breaching the surface like hairy submarines. They didn't seem to notice her, but they did notice food.

'Oh no you don't,' she said, backing away quickly as they clambered out of the pool and galloped towards her – muddy, food-seeking missiles. When fresh grass was hard to come by, the keepers added fruit, vegetables and a few scoops of grain to their diet, but supplies were short this week. There should still be apples and carrots, though. She held the enclosure gate shut with one foot and leaned over to open the apple store, scooping a dozen into her bucket. Hauling herself upright again, she released the gate just long enough to shift the bucket into both hands, gasping as the scraggly rump of one of the young boars flashed past her at a gallop.

'No!' she shouted, slamming the gate. 'Stop!'

The capy disappeared off towards the east gate of the zoo. Lucy clasped one hand over her mouth and cast about in dismay. Allowing an animal to escape was the most capital of crimes. What if someone found out before she could get him back? What if Luke found out and she lost her job?

Oh God, oh God, oh God. There was no way she could risk chasing around the perimeter of the zoo. Someone would see her and wonder what had happened. And she'd never catch him on her own anyway.

Lucy took a deep breath. OK. Something would occur to her. Maybe he'd come back of his own volition when he got hungry. Maybe some member of the public would capture him. She felt a terrible wave of despair. Poor thing had lived all of his short life in captivity; he wouldn't have a clue how to forage for food. And what if a dog found him? He may weigh as much as a grown man, Lucy thought, but he's still a rodent. Oh, Lord help me, she thought. Help me find him before someone else does.

That night, Lucy climbed into bed, too agitated to sleep. She thought of talking to God, her God – a benign, all-seeing sort of deity who didn't get too involved with the day-to-day running of life, but who (she imagined) liked to be kept informed – a sort of thoughtful, philosophy professor of a god, passing his days in contemplation of the moral complexities of good and evil.

'O dear Lord, what a day I've had,' she said to her idea of God. 'I've met a man and may have lost my job too. Actually, he's more of a boy. A boy-man. And an animal escaped. A capybara. Which is not good. But I'd quite like it if something more came of the meeting. With the person.' She broke off. 'Something meaningful. That isn't just a bit of fun, if you get my drift.' Here she paused, wanting to be precise. 'It would be so nice not to have to be alone all the time. And although we were only together for a few minutes, I felt something, a connection. I'm not talking about sex, exactly, it was more like . . . *wham*! *Lightning*.' She paused again. 'Not that no one's ever been interested in me before, and I do appreciate looking nice and all, but sometimes I get fed up with it – people just thinking, Woo hoo, she's hot.'

Perhaps, she thought, it would be best if she didn't go into the whole thing about leering boys with the Holy Father. 'I hope you don't mind my pointing out that it does put people off sometimes. Not that I'm complaining.' Was she? 'It's just that people seem not to see me sometimes. See *me*, that is, the real me.'

She lay silent for a few minutes. 'It's such a mess inside my head. I can't stop thinking about him. What if I never see him again? What if I never meet anyone I love?' She sighed. 'Or who loves me? And what about the capybara? That's such a disaster.'

Lucy exhaled and shut her eyes. 'I'm going to be in deep trouble if I don't get him back. I can't tell you how much I'd appreciate some help before anyone notices he's gone.' She screwed up her face, thinking hard, as if the choice had been put to her. 'I mean, if I had to choose, the capybara's probably more important in the short term and, really, I hate to be selfish, but in the long term?' That face, those eyes.

'Amen,' she said quickly, and, embarrassed by the absurdity of her theological monologue, pulled the covers up over her head.

Even on her own she felt self-conscious talking to God. But it made her feel better to talk, the way some people wrote in a journal. She didn't suppose God was listening to her, alone, and she wasn't so deluded or selfish that she imagined other people hadn't far bigger claims on God's time. But she felt better knowing that something (besides humans) was *there*. Not that faith was exactly easy. There were so many complications involved in belief, so many abstractions. And faith was so difficult to maintain in the absence of . . . of anything besides faith.

He hadn't even told her his surname. It was ludicrous to imagine anything other than a momentary spark between them. But . . . what did it mean that he seemed to know her, *her name*, even? And that whenever she closed her eyes she *saw* him? That face. She waited for the vision of him in her brain to fade, but waking and sleeping he was *there*. He haunted her.

Perhaps this was what love felt like. She could almost hear his voice whispering her name, feel his hands on her face, pulling her lips towards his. Her imagination conjured the caress of his hand on her hip and then . . . *oh*! The sensation so real!

Without sleep, tomorrow would be hopeless. Her job required so much attention to detail; she couldn't afford mistakes. *More* mistakes. The capybara's disappearing rump filled her head. Sleep! Lucy closed her eyes and tried to think of something nice, transporting herself to a warm beach on a summer's day, with seagulls and waves and the sun flowing down. She relaxed each muscle one by one, starting with her toes and her feet and her ankles, letting the weight of her body sink into the soft place created by her mind; she could almost feel the trickling sand between her fingers. She sank lower and lower towards sleep; waves of drowsiness lulled her softly, like long strokes of a hand, slowly, lower and lower, two hands now, each cupping a buttock and then moving, edging carefully down between her . . .

Oh my giddy aunt, she thought, shooting upright in the dark. He's here! I can actually feel his *fingers*! She flipped sideways off the bed in the dark, hauling the covers with her as she fell. Crouching, heart pounding, she flicked on the bedside lamp, fully expecting to see an intruder standing by the bed.

But there was nothing. Of course there was nothing. What would there be? Feeling foolish, Lucy switched off the light and crawled back into bed.

'Jesus,' she murmured. 'What's wrong with me? I'm going stark raving mad.'

Bob smiled at her, tenderly, from the dark.

16

Bob had recently taken to considering questions of great spiritual complexity. What was it that made one transcendently beautiful girl different from another? Why did he begin to ache with helpless need when a certain face combined with a certain outline? What message ran from his bollocks to his brain to say, 'Yes! It is she!'

Even God couldn't answer that one.

'Eck?' Eck peered at Bob's breakfast. Bob might go hours and days without eating and then consume an entire week's food at a single sitting. Now, he finished a dozen doughnuts, throwing the empty box to Eck.

There was so much to do. He needed to have sex with Lucy, get a replacement pet and find himself a mother who lived much, much further away.

He sat for quite some time, wondering how he might make all of these things happen.

Mr B was the obvious answer, of course. He hated to admit it, but he depended on Mr B, who busied himself with the stuff that Bob found boring, the day-to-day banal stuff, the general running of the world. It was great to be able to delegate politics and social issues (humanity, in general) to someone who could be bothered to deal with it, while he exerted his energy in the appreciation of his more delightful creations.

This thought led him to wonder why he hadn't made every woman on Earth in the image of Lucy, why he'd insisted on infinite variety. Perhaps it had been simple carelessness? Now that he thought about it, why hadn't he specified that all women had skin as soft and smooth as warm almond oil? He hadn't really considered it a priority at the time, and for a while the beasts of the field had taken up all his energy. Now, however, he realized how short-sighted he'd been. Had he really needed a beaver? A coelacanth? Wouldn't a world full of Lucys have been so much pleasanter than hoverflies and worms?

There was nothing he could do about it now, but he'd definitely be more careful in his next job. When this planet shut down, they'd give him another, and next time he'd fill it with achingly gorgeous girls, all desperate to have sex with him. Where was the downside?

In the meantime, he needed to focus, sort out the practicalities. A serious move on Lucy was required, and soon. One, because he would go mad if he didn't have sex with her. And two, because his loony mother was probably, right now, setting some insidious trap that would take nine hundred and ninety-nine per cent of his time and energy to evade.

He considered the options. Annunciation had been known to work. White robes, big wings, spooky lighting, golden halo. All he had to do was appear to the object of passion and make some sort of pronouncement. 'You have been chosen by God.' Full stop. Resist the temptation to elaborate.

Such an approach was particularly effective with women inclined to the ecstatic – nuns, seers, religious martyrs – but in these secular times he wondered whether it might not lead to shock, violent rejection or arrest. Things were different back then. Once, he'd appeared to a particularly edible girl as a swan. He couldn't remember why. Another time, as a bull. What a laugh. Good times!

Let's face it, he'd eked some serious mileage out of the God thing. Getting that old guy to drag his son up a mountain? Cool! Smiting of the first born? Yes! Turning the errant into pillars of salt? Fun! Once upon a time it had been all burning bushes, plagues of frogs and partings of the seas, scaring the living daylights out of his creations by booming down in scary voices and handing stone tablets out of the sky. Now he was barely allowed to make a parking space become suddenly available.

It was all Mr B's fault. The Crackdown, he called it. One joke too many. Just because of a few harmless pranks.

The guy had zero sense of humour.

So it was all rinky-dink stuff now, stuff that he could slip past B, who had taken to watching him like a hawk. Could life *get* any worse?

Bob ground his teeth. He'd have to be stealthy, devise a cunning plan. Adrenalin inspired a series of unworkably complex schemes. Mr B would be expecting something along his usual lines – a gigantic chimera or a dragon. So he'd confound him. Become a cat, a stray cat, a stray *tom*cat. Lucy would adopt him. And then, one night, while he lay on her knee rumbling with contentment, he'd lift her skirt with his paw . . .

Or he'd put Mr B off the scent. Transform himself into something small and innocuous. A spider. An ant. Eck! He'd disguise himself as Eck and steal away to seek his beloved. No one would ever suspect Eck of anything. Reaching Lucy, he would clamber up on to her lap and she would caress him gently, while his long sticky tongue explored her . . .

The thought depressed him. Who'd want to have sex with Eck anyway? Depressing little creature.

I know, thought Bob. I'll invite her to dinner!

It was so straightforward. He snorted with contempt. Mr B would never think of a plan like that. He, however, was God, and God was perfectly capable of writing to his beloved, a simple note requesting her presence at a designated time and place. He thought for a moment. They could always meet at the zoo, at closing time. Easy as pie. They would meet at the exit to the zoo and they would have a meal, and then she would take him back to her apartment where they would gaze into each other's eyes and hold hands and touch lips and possibly, with a little luck and a following wind, indulge in a few rounds of incredibly romantic rumpy pumpy ding dong merrily on high.

This was exactly the sort of situation Mr B should be working on day and night for him, *facilitating*. And he could do it too. Bob knew that it was easily within his capabilities. He'd know exactly what to write in a note that might be slipped into a mailbox or under a door, which door to slip it under, what paper to use, what tone to take. So why didn't he? He did what Bob asked (reluctantly, and with a good deal of foot-dragging), but what good was that? Bob hated

68

asking. *Take the initiative*, he wanted to shout. Think about what might make *me* happy for a change, then do it *as a surprise*. Asking all the time was such a pain.

Dear Lucy (read the note). He paused for a long moment. *Dear Lucy*. He tapped the pen on the table. *Dear Lucy* was a good clear start. Not *Dearest Lucy*. No, short was better. Short and to the point. *Dear Lucy*. He thought for a minute. *Please meet me at the exit to the zoo at closing time next Tuesday. Yours sincerely, Bob.*

As an afterthought, he added, *Remember me? I'm the guy who helped you walk the llama.*

He read it to Eck, who confirmed it as a great literary masterpiece.

Bob sat back, delighted. What woman could resist an invitation from God written in so persuasive a manner? There was authority, majesty even, in the prose. Lucy couldn't fail to notice.

The thought of seeing her again made him giddy. Was it possible that after all these years he had finally found a woman who would love him for his real true self? The him with emotions and feelings and needs beyond all that Supreme Ruler stuff? He licked the edge of the envelope, wrote 'Lucy' in big letters on the outside and gave it to Eck, who diligently padded off across town, slipped through the front gate of the zoo and under the door of the staff offices, placed it carefully inside Lucy's locker, polished off the packet of custard creams and a jarful of instant coffee granules by the employee kettle and returned home.

So, that was that. Now it was dark. Nearly midnight. Bob threw himself down on his bed. If he went to bed now, he'd wake all refreshed and renewed, bright as a button in time to meet his beloved after work next Tuesday.

On a whim, he nipped out to check on her, proud of holding back the steamroller of his love. He'd show his mother and that annoying Mr B that he was perfectly capable of having a proper relationship with a human.

Hours later, the sensation of Lucy's silky skin still lingered on his fingertips. How on earth was he supposed to sleep with so much anticipation churning in his brain, so much longing in his soul? Not to mention the terror of wondering whether his mother might suddenly ambush him again, demanding he accompany her to a game of tiddlywinks, at which he would lose his planet/sanity/the shirt off his back. He summoned Eck and put him on guard duty.

Bob tossed and turned for several long seconds before he slept. Eck stayed awake for the rest of the night, thinking about being dead.

17

Mr B received notice that his resignation had been received. *Thank you for your correspondence*, read the standardized letter. *We accept your request for termination with regret, and shall respond to your application for a new job by the end of your notice period.* Some bureaucrat had scribbled *July 14th* in the blank space below.

He stared at the bit of paper. Was that it? All the worry and careful planning, the excruciating care with which he'd made his decision, drafted and organized his thoughts . . . for a form letter? He would have experienced more outrage had he not been so relieved.

He rechecked the date on the form. The fourteenth of July. Less than six weeks. Not so long in the scheme of eternity.

Mr B dreamt of the planet he would go to next, a planet he could love, one that was orderly, sane and free of despair. But could he really leave? Could he simply fly off to some new challenge without a care in the world, shouting a last 'So long, suckers!' to all the oppressed species of Earth? Could he leave them to Bob with a clear conscience, with any sort of conscience at all? Had they even read his meticulous files, the catalogue of malpractice compiled across years of personal suffering? His letter had been a work of thorough documentation and well-reasoned pathos, driven by a keen (if he said so himself) intellectual rigour and a hopeful heart. Did anyone notice that Earth had been so mismanaged? Did anyone (but him) care? And what about his whales? Could he skip happily off without a backwards glance, leaving their fate to Bob?

He thought he probably could.

A glass of wine, a nice lunch of melted Gruyère on toast (the crusts for Eck), and he returned to work. There was a rhythm to the toil, a repetition that might have been soothing had the narrative not been so relentlessly grim: Babies and Battles, Brittle Bones and Baseball. ('*O merciful Lord in heaven, hear my prayer, let the opposing team contract a short-term, moderately debilitating illness that does not become evident until the seventh inning, O Lord, bad enough to allow us to win the game, the series and the championship without undue suspicion being cast in the matter of divine intervention, thank you very much, yours sincerely, etc., etc., amen.*')

The number of petitions loomed perilously close to infinite; the number of miracles Mr B could effect, pitifully low. His head hurt. Cancer. Concentration camps. Congo, Democratic Republic of, complete with exploitation by European settlers, relentless elimination of indigenous people, warlords and election irregularities, government corruption, famine, disease, ecological crises. And rape. Ninety-year-old women, one-month-old babies. Each day, a new crisis, a new massacre, a new threat of extinction, disease, internecine conflict, meteorological catastrophe.

Well, what do you expect when you skip through Creation in six lousy days?

Very creative, yes indeed. And now, as usual, *he* had to pick it apart. Day after day, strand by bloody strand, coaxing the Gordian knot to loosen its grip, begging and hoping it into submission.

Mr B shook his head. Behold man. Violent, self-serving and ruthless when in power; exploited, miserable and diseased when not. On the one hand there was slavery, war, inquisition and ethnic cleansing; on the other, Shakespeare, chocolate, the Taj Mahal. A fine balance.

Whales. He called up an abstract of International Whaling Commission guidelines, read it through, found the cross-reference to the actual petitioners taking issue (who could blame them?) with regulated harvest and the destruction of the oceans. 'Regulated harvest'. What a charming alternative to 'murder'.

The latest crisis was contamination, a potent cocktail of herbicides, fungicides and pesticides that poisoned the groundwater that poisoned the sea. And so the whales set off, the ones that remained, circling the globe in an increasingly desperate search for more congenial waters, a sea that they remembered from long ago as safe and welcoming.

Oh, the whales, thought Mr B, the poor whales.

He contemplated folders and boxes, Post-it notes stuck to his desk, a stack of coloured files piled to the ceiling, a to-do list with the ancient neglected appearance of a holy relic. Could he clear all this before he left?

He sighed. Of course he couldn't. But he was determined to make a final stand, to guarantee the safety of his whales before he waved goodbye to the whole miserable enterprise.

He placed both hands over his ears in an attempt to shut out the sudden pounding of hailstones on his window and then looked up, startled. Hail, in a heat wave? A knot of dread began to form in his bowels.

Here we go, he thought, it's starting. Sex weather – excited, confused, arousal weather. How many times over the centuries had he experienced this development as a prelude to catastrophe? Mr B could not pretend that this was just some ordinary climatic variation. He recognized Bob's presence behind the sudden peculiarly urgent change of weather.

God help us, Mr B thought. With no actual hope that he would.

18

'What'cha doing?'

'What do I appear to be doing?' Mr B replied mildly. 'I'm dedicating every minute of my life, as usual, to the futile pursuit of order. I am but a humble fisherman engaged in the hopeless task of unravelling the frantic net of despair you have cast upon the victims of your creativity.'

Bob rolled his eyes. 'Yes, but *aside* from that. I mean what are you doing right now? Because I need advice.'

'A bit late for that, buddy boy. I could have offered oodles of advice back when you were playing 52 Pick-Up with alphabet spaghetti and calling it creation. But would you take advice then?'

'*Hello?*'

Mr B paused. Put down his pen. Rubbed his aching forehead. 'What can I do for you?'

'You spend all your time worrying about people you don't even know. And you don't ever stop to wonder whether I'm suffering too.'

'Are you?' Mr B raised an eyebrow. 'Well, I *am* sorry. Do tell.' Eck had crept on to his desk and was attempting to pocket a teacake. Mr B picked the cake up and replaced it on the plate. Eck snapped at his hand and missed.

The boy folded his arms across his chest and turned away. 'I'm not going to tell you now.'

'Excellent. If we're finished, then perhaps I could get back to work.'

Bob stamped his foot. 'You never pay attention to me! You don't care about anyone other than those poxy poor people in your poxy files.' He put on a nyah-nyah whine. '*Oh, look at me, I've got AIDS, I was in a war, my baby's dead.* If you're so worried about them, why don't you go live in the bloody Democratic bloody Republic of Tonga –'

'Congo.'

'*Bloody* Democratic *bloody* Republic of *bloody stupid-arse Congo.*'

Mr B regarded him dispassionately. 'How can I help?'

'Lucy.'

'Not again.'

'No, not *again*. We're in love.'

'In love? Sounds idyllic. So what's the trouble?' I know what mine is, Mr B thought. Every time you fall in love, my problems increase exponentially.

Bob squirmed and looked away. 'I want to have sex with her. Be with her. You know, the proper way.' The expression on his face softened.

If, after their many millennia of togetherness, Mr B had retained even an ounce of interest in Bob's emotional struggles, he might have experienced a twinge of sympathy. 'The proper way? And what way would that be?'

Bob's mouth twisted, his eyes glittered with unshed tears. 'You know. Flowers and love songs and that. Like *they* do it.'

'They, *humans*?' Mr B remembered another girl, another time, with the face of an angel and the sweetest manners, a child's soft mouth and an expression open and trusting as a lamb. She had seen Bob for what he was, and loved him anyway. Mr B removed his spectacles, hoping to erase the vision in his head. That romance had ended with floods, tornadoes, plague, earthquakes and the girl's execution for heresy, a few weeks before her fourteenth birthday. By special order of Pope Urban II.

Bob nodded.

'Well, you can't have it both ways. You can't be a god and live like a human. What are you going to do once you fall in love the "proper way"? Buy a nice suburban bungalow? Work in an office? Go to barbecues?'

'I don't think you understand.' Bob's tone was icy. 'Lucy and I are going to be together forever. We're getting married.'

'Together forever?' Mr B felt a little wild. 'Do you even know what that word means? If you hadn't created humans to grow old, die and rot in less time than it takes you to get dressed most mornings, *then* maybe you could have been together forever. But you and Lucy will *not* be together for anything remotely resembling forever. It's not possible.'

Bob said nothing. He gazed into the middle distance, looking wounded.

'Look.' This conversation was proving tiresome, and Mr B had work to do. 'Why not take her out for a meal, see how it goes and then make another date? Take it one step at a time. Deal with this week before you get on to eternity.'

Bob rolled his eyes. 'Oh, thank you. Fantastic advice. Thank you *so* much.'

'It might go down better than appearing to her as a giant reptile encased in a ball of fire and forcing yourself on her.'

'*Why do you always have to bring that up?* Why don't you just leave me alone?' Bob stormed out, slamming the front door behind him.

Thunder crashed. Electric rain fell in sheets.

19

'Daddy, I've become very attached to him.'

Her father didn't look up. 'That's unfortunate.'

'Nevertheless.' Estelle paused. 'I'd very much prefer it if you didn't eat him.'

Hed sat with a calculator, adding up figures. 'All well and good for you, but what about my wager? What if I start not collecting debts? Then what? Everyone and his penguin will be wanting an exception.' He looked at her. 'I'm sorry, but I can't be having that. Who'll keep you in frocks then?'

Frocks? Estelle looked at him.

He sighed, impatient. 'What do you propose I do? Tell Mona it was all a mistake? That a debt is not a debt?' His eyes softened. 'Of course, she is a good-looking woman. Funny how you can sit across a poker table from someone all these years . . .' Looking up, he saw Estelle staring at him thoughtfully. In an instant his face clouded with anger, and he brought his fist down on the table. 'No! No exceptions. And no more bothering me.'

Estelle waited for a very long time, unmoving, as he continued with his sums. She was not a girl to waste valuable time that might better have been spent thinking. 'I'm not saying you should cancel the debt,' she said at last, and then paused. 'But I have an idea.'

Her father sighed again. 'What sort of an idea?'

'A good one. It involves accepting something. In lieu.'

Hed's eyes were black and as fathomless as eternity. 'That won't do.'

'Surely that depends on what the something is.' They stared each other down. 'Daddy, for heaven's sake. You don't really want to eat the Eck, do you? I'm certain Mona just made that up about how delicious he is.'

'I hope, for her sake, that she didn't.'

Estelle's gaze remained steady. Hed thought he detected the flicker of a smile. He sat back in his chair and crossed his arms. 'Stop beating about the bush. Let's hear.'

'No,' she said. 'Not yet.'

He shrugged. 'Suit yourself. But what makes you think I'll find your plan acceptable?'

'Nothing,' she said.

There was a beat, and then Hed's face broke into a smile like the sun coming out from behind a cloud. He sat back in his chair and gazed at his daughter admiringly.

'You're a girl after my own heart, Estelle. Shame I can't convince you to play poker. You'd wipe the floor with us all.'

Estelle's mouth curled ever so slightly upward. 'I may do that anyway.'

20

Mr B found himself alone one minute and not the next. On a chair opposite him, Mona squeezed greyish water from the crocheted doily that comprised her dress.

'Oh! Hello, my darling. What appalling weather. How on earth do you manage to survive on this dreary little planet?'

Mr B shivered, though not with the cold. 'Yes,' he said. 'It's been terrible.' Increasingly terrible. Rain, storms at sea, thunder, gale-force winds – every violent nasty element you might expect to follow one of Bob's tantrums. If he didn't get together with Lucy soon, they'd all be blown away, struck by lightning or drowned.

And if he did? B sighed. It would probably be worse.

Mona examined his office. 'So, this is where you've been hiding.'

'Hiding, Mona?' He raised an eyebrow. 'How very nice to see you again.' Bob's mother was living proof that self-centred fecklessness could be inherited, but he couldn't quite bring himself to dislike her.

She peered at him. 'Darling, you look tired. Are you working too hard?'

'Of course not.' Of course not? He smiled. 'You, on the other hand, look lovely as ever.'

She exhaled deeply. 'To be perfectly honest, I feel a bit down.'

'Oh?'

'Bob's terribly cross with me for gambling away his pet.'

Mr B tried to look sympathetic while Eck, who had been standing under the desk, poked his head out a few centimetres and peered up. 'Eck?'

He patted the little creature absently. 'I thought you'd given up gambling.'

'It was wrong, darling. I know that now.'

Mr B looked thoughtful. 'I don't think we can allow him to . . .' He briefly mimed bringing a fork to his mouth.

'No, no, of course not. I'll figure something out. I'm certain Hed will be willing to compromise.'

Under the table, a gleam of hope lit Eck's small black eyes, but what little Mr B knew of Emoto Hed made him think that Mona's certainty was misplaced.

'And even if he won't, I've told Bob I'd get him another pet. Ten more. But he's not having it. So unreasonable!' She wrung her hands. 'I know he's my own son, darling, but I hope you'll excuse my saying that he can be impossibly stubborn. It must be dreadful for you, sharing a life with him. And it's all my fault.' Mona appeared genuinely contrite. 'But, you see, I was just trying to be a good mother.'

'Of course, Mona.'

'And any day now, Bob will rise to the challenge.'

It had been approximately ten thousand years. To Mr B, this seemed sufficient notice to rise to most occasions.

He smiled, a little tightly. 'Perhaps he will. But in the meantime I could very much do with some help.'

She brightened. 'I am utterly at your service, my dear. Just say the word.'

Mr B said a great number of words. He told Mona about Bob and Lucy and the weather. He told her about the state of his nerves and the despair he felt for Bob's creations. And then he took a deep breath, and told her that he had handed in his notice.

Mona's hands flew to her mouth. 'Oh, my heavens!' she cried. 'You've resigned? But you can't resign! You can't leave Bob to run the planet on his own.'

Mr B frowned. 'He *is* God.'

She waved dismissively. 'Yes, well, he may be God, but just between you and me, he's not much of a God.' She sighed. 'He's hopeless, in fact. You know it, and I know it, and all of his miserable little creations know it.'

Mr B examined the upper left-hand corner of the room.

'You're serious this time, aren't you?' Her eyes shimmered with tears.

He nodded.

'But how will he manage alone, poor thing?'

'If you'll excuse my saying, Mona, it's not Bob so much I'm worried about.'

'Oh, I see.' Mona's eyes overflowed. 'But you have to make allowances; the poor boy's suffered terribly.'

Mr B raised an eyebrow.

She sniffed. 'He's nearly an orphan.'

As Mr B understood the word 'orphan', being *nearly* one was tantamount to not being one at all. And if (by chance) some question remained, Bob's status as orphan seemed disadvantaged by his mother's presence here today. As for his father . . . Mona might not know which of her many lovers he was, but chances were he was still alive and kicking.

'Well,' she said, pulling out a small notepad, 'I shall certainly put my mind to the Bob problem. Just remind me what's required? Let's see. One: make Bob a better God. Two: get him to stop playing with mortals. Three: no more floods, rain, natural disasters, etc. etc. and four . . .' She raised an eyebrow in the direction of the Eck. 'No et-P-ay for inner-D-ay.'

Mr B blinked.

'Right. Is that everything? Yes? Excellent. Now don't you worry, my darling. Mona will take care of everything.' And then she was gone.

Once more, he wondered what would happen next.

'Eck.' The noise from knee level was mournful. Mr B reached under the desk and patted Bob's doomed pet. With a sigh, he opened a drawer and pulled out some ancient peanuts in a cellophane packet. Eck snaffled them up with his flexible nose and scuttled off into the corner to eat them. Mr B watched him.

Until the poker game, he had been quite a feisty little soul, falling upon food each time with a glorious bleat of joy. He was a different Eck now that his life had been truncated, and who could blame him? Each meal he ate was one closer to his last. This was not an easy concept to swallow. Being mortal, he would, of course, have died eventually, but now he knew exactly when, and why, and (to an unpleasant extent) how. Now, every tick of the clock brought him closer to oblivion.

Mr B felt depressed. Another doomed creature he couldn't help.

When next he checked, the little beast was asleep, his empty peanut packet cradled in his arms like a baby.

21

Newspapers reported the worst spring weather in the history of spring weather. The rain seemed to have developed a personality of its own – sharp and vindictive one minute, heavy and morose the next. So peevish was the mood that it might have been programmed by some gigantic, love-struck, miserable, sulking teenager.

Which, of course, it was.

Low-lying areas began to flood. Plastic bottles floated and bumped in casual rafts accompanied by the sordid ghosts of billowing carrier bags. Defunct sandbags sagged against doorframes; shop owners pressed gaffer tape on to window frames. Filthy water fed the sewers, which fed the canals, which fed the rivers and the bay, and ran eventually into the sea.

And still it rained.

At not yet ten in the morning, the vicar of St Christopher's church stared out of the window of his office while speaking emphatically and with some volume down the telephone.

Outside, the water was still rising; police and coastguard teams occupied themselves in the relocation of vulnerable citizens. Large pieces of furniture floated by, while individual articles of clothing hovered just below the surface, appearing and disappearing according to the movements of whirlpools. A pair of boys, balancing golf umbrellas between their knees, paddled an orange inflatable, peering into the windows of abandoned shops and flats as they passed.

Looking for loot, Bernard thought. Nice.

A dog swam past the window searching for somewhere to rest. He scrambled up on to a windowsill and lay with his thin heaving chest and front paws clinging to the ledge while his rear end still churned away, treading water. Poor old thing, mused the vicar, he won't last long there. And, sure enough, after a minute he was off again, paddling doggedly downstream past a long row of shops, searching for solid ground, in vain. Maybe the boys would find him and pull him on board their boat, make him some sort of mascot.

Maybe they wouldn't, and he'd drown.

'I haven't a clue what to do with these people.' Speaking slowly, to encourage comprehension at the other end, Bernard attempted to keep the impatience out of his voice. 'We've run out of Weetabix and coffee and blankets. And nappies and loo paper. And sanitary towels. The toilets are flooded so we're resorting to buckets, there isn't enough bedding to go around and the children are howling. There's tea and shortbread, but I don't dare put it out. We'd have a riot.'

He listened for a long moment.

'Well, yes, of course I understand, but . . .' He broke off at the sight of a large green reptile advancing on his office.

Mrs Laura Davenport had donned her husband's fly-fishing waders, jacket and oilskin hat to walk the mile from her home to St Christopher's church. She smiled at her old friend and tilted her head away from the phone conversation, assuming an expression of not listening.

She'd known Bernard since university and he'd barely changed since then – still slim and lanky, his face full of humour, almost no grey in the dark hair that fell over his eyes like a schoolboy's. Laura Davenport, although happy enough with her lawyer husband, had married her second choice. She would never acknowledge (least of all to herself) that twenty-five years later this remained a source of regret.

When at last Bernard put down the phone, her feet were cold and she longed for a nice hot cup of tea. Not that it would be proper to ask, of course. So many parishioners stranded. For her to have a house on a hill, dry furniture *and* a cup of tea might be considered one blessing too many.

She kissed his cheek and offered her best sympathetic frown-smile. 'No support from headquarters, then?'

Bernard shook his head. 'None whatsoever. They're up to their eyes in their own mess. Hail today, have you heard? Hailstones like cricket balls. Big enough to smash windows.' He exhaled slowly. 'In the meantime, we've got too many refugees and the Met Office is three forecasts behind. I get the distinct impression that even the Red Cross couldn't give a stuff about a parish church full of stranded locals.' He met Laura's eyes and smiled wearily. 'Hail. Whatever next?'

'Perhaps it's a sign.'

'Of . . .?'

Laura laughed. 'You tell me. You're the one with God's ear.'

'God's ear?' He winced. 'I can barely get the dean to take my calls.'

'I suppose it's quite appropriate when you think of it. St Christopher's providing respite for all these weary travellers.'

'God works in mysterious ways,' said Bernard. 'I've been thinking of tossing a dove out to see what it brings back.'

'You're not the first person to mention Noah. The papers are full of it.'

'It's my fault. Not the water, the people. I've got a boat, you see.'

Laura stared. 'A *boat*? You have a boat?'

He nodded happily. 'A little Zodiac. Worth more than my pension the way things are now. I've been sneaking out in it to bring back supplies.'

'And refugees?'

He shrugged. 'Only the most desperate. I'm gathering them two by two. Or three.'

'What a dark horse you are, Bernard. I should have known you'd turn up with a boat. But how on earth?'

'I won it in a raffle. Years ago. Kept it in my garage. Nearly forgot I had it. The funny thing is that it works. Lovely little putt-putt engine, just drained some petrol out of the car, mixed it with oil and off we went. Its range is limited by the flood, of course.'

'You *are* a clever man. Do you mean I might have left Andrew's fishing boots at home?'

'Of course.'

She unfastened the clips on her shoulders, stripped the rubber bib down and shimmied her way out of the waist-high rubber suit. 'Ugh,' she said. 'My amphibian days are over.'

'I'm almost sorry to hear that.'

'No you're not,' she said sternly. 'Now, come along, Bernard. You need to find something strenuous for me to accomplish.'

Bernard peered into the large shopping bag she'd left by the door. 'This is a good start,' he said, perusing the contents. There was a box of PG Tips, two packets of rice and six cans of baked beans, but Bernard wasn't as certain about the rest – chickpeas, gentleman's relish, mustard, a jar of tomato chutney with a handwritten label, jelly (lemon and raspberry), four bottles of Indian tonic, one large box of novelty teabags (apricot, grapefruit medley and green apple), half a bag of sultanas, an open packet of cream crackers, some icing sugar, organic dried mangoes, salad cream, a Christmas pudding, cans of herrings and smoked oysters.

'I'm sorry there's not more,' she said. 'But we're getting down to the bottom of the cupboard ourselves.' She peered at the sad selection of leftovers. 'It wasn't easy getting out of the house with this. Andrew loves smoked oysters.'

'How is Andrew?' Bernard asked, but they both knew the question didn't require an answer. Andrew was always fine. 'I don't like to go on about shortages in front of the parishioners. But I can't figure out how we're going to feed them.'

'You're doing the best you can.'

'No.' Bernard felt disheartened. Sometimes he was convinced that God only answered the prayers of the young and healthy, the ones who asked for love, or to get what they wanted for Christmas, or to pass their exams. For the disillusioned middle-aged or the elderly, it struck him as just one hopeless petition after another. 'Please, God, help my husband love me again.' 'Cure my wife's dementia.' 'Make the children stop taking drugs.' Even he didn't believe that sort of prayer would be answered.

Laura looked down at the bows of her tidy patent-leather shoes. She wasn't entirely keen on Bernard's dejection, preferring him stalwart and rendered cheerful by the Lord. 'Come along,' she said. 'Let's see what we can do for the rabble.' As she followed him out of the tiny office, her thoughts strayed to a wholly involuntary image of the vicar pushing her back across his desk, her sensible tweed skirt ruched up round her hips. She shook her head to banish it.

'How's my Lucy?' asked Bernard, leading her through to the nave.

'Still tending the animals, still a virgin.'

'*Laura.*'

'Well, it's very worrying to think one's daughter might never find a man worthy of her ridiculously high standards.'

'Of course she will. She's just particular.'

'I'm sure you're right, but really, Bernard, you should try my job for a week. Mother of daughters.'

Since childhood, Laura's younger child had been as religious as her sister was stubbornly secular, always turning the other cheek and maintaining a firm grip on her moral values. Laura had intermittently worried that this was what came of making Bernard Lucy's godfather.

Of course there was nothing wrong with a modicum of Christian faith; it could even be considered a good and proper attribute for a young girl to possess. But as to its *degree*, well, you could understand why Laura and her husband worried. As young as six or seven, Lucy had been prone to visitations by angels, great winged apparitions that came nightly to sit on her bed. Neither parent knew exactly how to react.

Bernard made it his business to reassure them, explaining that the more powerful imagery of religion often caught the imaginations of small children and hardly ever led to an actual wedding to Christ, but Laura worried. Angels? Whatever next?

She emerged from her thoughts to find Bernard waiting, hand on the door to the main hall. 'Coming, Laura?'

She nodded.

As he opened the door, the milling crowd of refugees looked up as one.

Behind him, Laura began unbuttoning her ivory sateen cuffs, folding them up neatly above her elbows in preparation for getting stuck in.

22

Bob settled down in bed with a bucket of junk food. He needed to relax, to figure out his next move. He was fading away, dying of love. The mere thought of Lucy was enough to make him feel faint.

'Eck,' moaned Eck softly in the region of Bob's left ear, followed by a little probing sweep of his tongue. *Sexy.*

Bob smacked him.

Eck squeaked, but a minute later had installed himself in the crook of Bob's elbow and was nibbling BBQ wings. Bob stroked him absentmindedly.

'Hello, my darling.'

Bob looked up, snorted and turned back to his meal. At his side, Eck had moved on to a party-sized bag of cheese balls. He swivelled one beady eye.

'I think what you meant to say was, "Hello, Mother, how wonderful to see you."'

'Go away.' Bob flapped a hand in her direction. 'Why are you here? To gamble away more of my possessions? Marry me off to a shovelful of dark matter? Sell tickets to my nightmares?'

Mona frowned. 'That's no way to talk to your loving

mother. You're getting on now, darling; it's time you learned a little respect.' She composed her face into an expression of stern reproach, held it for a long moment, then relaxed and beamed at him. 'There. All done. You know me, petal, not one to hold a grudge.'

'That makes one of us. Look at poor Eck.' They both stared down at the little penguiny creature, who obediently switched on his mournful expression. 'Hasn't had a moment's peace since his death sentence.'

'He's got a reprieve.'

'Oh yes, how could I forget. His *reprieve*. Lucky, *lucky*, Eck. How long was it again? Forever? Oh no, wait. Six weeks. Less than five now. Nearly as good.'

'No need for sarcasm.' Mona frowned, a little peevishly. 'I know I did wrong, but I was hoping you might find it in your heart to forgive –'

'Please, stop, Mother. I am immune to your repellent displays of emotion.'

His mother shook her head sadly. 'Oh, Bob, darlingest boy, how very little you understand the depths of a mother's love.'

'Blah blah blah.'

Mona sighed. Was it her imagination, or was everyone on a mission to make her feel guilty all of a sudden? 'So, he's not pleased with his reprieve?'

Bob waved a hand at Eck. 'What do you think? Not long till . . .' He drew a finger along his neck. 'Din-dins.'

The Eck's eyes shot open, wide with terror.

'Speaking of which,' Mona's eyes slid sideways, 'I'm afraid you're going to have to stay away from that girl.'

'Speaking of what?' Bob's jaw dropped. 'What's she got to do with you? *Why* have I got to?'

Mona reached for his hand, which he snatched away. 'Aren't you being just a teensy bit selfish, my darling?'

'Selfish?' His eyes widened. '*I'm* selfish? You gamble away my pet's life in a poker game and you call *me* selfish?'

He stood glaring, while Mona's huge eyes telegraphed reproach. She sighed.

'Darlingest boy, let's not fight. I know I haven't been a perfect mother. But right now I simply want you to leave the girl alone. She's human. It won't work. And, according to Mr B, you're halfway to destroying the biosphere.'

From his place at Bob's elbow, Eck made kissy noises. Bob whacked him, pouting. 'I'm in love.'

'But honey-bunch, every time you fall in love, it ends in a firestorm. You lose interest, you ruin some poor girl's life, Earth erupts in natural disasters, millions die.' She traced the path of an imaginary tear down one perfect cheek. 'It saddens me.'

'How do you even know what happens in my life?'

'I read the papers, sweetheart. I keep in touch.'

'Papers? *What papers?*'

Mona waved a dismissive hand. 'People talk.'

'*Which people?*' Bob's head spun with exasperation. 'Look, why don't you explain why you've suddenly developed an interest in my social life, and then bugger off.'

'Darling. It's because I'm your mother.'

'*And?*'

'It's only . . .' She smiled, a sad little smile. 'It's just that you're getting a teensy-weensy bit of a reputation.'

Bob goggled at her. '*What's that got to do with you?*'

'Oh, sweetheart, you know how it is. Mothers always get blamed. It's not fair, obviously, but . . . *I* got you the job so *I'm* at fault. Ridiculous, obviously, but . . .' She shrugged.

He pressed both hands to his ears. 'I cannot *believe* what I am hearing. I'm ruining *your* reputation?'

Mona looked mournful. 'No mother likes to hear bad things said about her children.'

'*What* bad things? What are you talking about? I've done incredibly well! *Everyone* thinks so!'

Mona looked away and studied her nails. 'If you say so, darling.'

'Look.' He struggled to regain control. 'If I'm so completely useless, how did I get to be God?'

Mona blinked, face arranged in an expression of genuine sympathy. 'Perhaps no one else wanted the job?'

Bob sat down hard. That possibility hadn't occurred to him.

23

Estelle was an unusually competent individual, unusually competent even for a goddess, and given that goddesses did not habitually enter human-style professions such as law, medicine or accountancy, an argument might be made for the fact that her fine intelligence and thoughtful sensibility were underexercised.

Of course Emoto Hed required a great deal of careful management, and as his only child Estelle had nearly a full-time job. Her first few thousand years had been spent in her own quiet campaign to get the measure of her father without inciting his easily incited wrath.

She had learned a great deal from their relationship. A great deal about sidestepping danger, about subtle man-oeuvring and oblique angles. She had learned the uses of persuasion, of silence, of a steady gaze; had learned to hold her nerve and not back down – without presenting herself as a challenge. She had learned, occasionally, to be sneaky.

If Estelle had been born human, she might have employed these talents as a diplomat or an international negotiator. As a goddess, however, she was jobless, had always been jobless, and could easily remain jobless throughout eternity.

There was no need, after all, for her to make a living. Surely the responsibilities of a dutiful child to a dangerously unstable father were occupation enough?

Estelle might have remained content with this existence had she never attended the fateful poker game, never met Eck, never witnessed Bob's heartbreaking incompetence as God of Earth. But having done all those things, she had noticed lately that something had changed. She, in fact, had changed.

For one thing, she had begun to wonder whether there was any point to her existence at all.

In this state of impatience, she began to travel. She travelled to happy planets, productive planets, gigantic watery planets and tiny dry ones, planets comprised almost exclusively of ice, planets designed by highly intelligent creatures, planets upon which every inhabitant had the imagination of a bath plug or the aesthetic appeal of a pile of dung. Most of the creatures she met could not easily be described in terms an Earth human would understand, for, contrary to common understanding, 'aliens' did not possess huge eyes and truncated human limbs, but took the form of vapours, shadows or nanoparticles, of fleeting thoughts, absences or false memories.

Estelle observed these many new places and nearly fell in love with many of them. But in the end, none needed her, or expressed much in the way of sadness when she left. So her feelings of emptiness persisted, despite the fact that her knowledge of the universe expanded considerably.

'Where are you off to now?' demanded her father as she prepared for yet another far-flung visit.

She kissed him. 'Nowhere in particular, Daddy.'

'And what's wrong with staying here and making my breakfast?'

'I've left instructions for your breakfast while I'm gone.'

'Hmph,' he growled. 'You won't find what you're looking for, you know. Particularly if you don't know what it is.'

Estelle stopped for a moment. 'Perhaps,' she said, with a small smile, 'I'll recognize it when I see it.'

'Nonsense,' rumbled her father. 'Tit over arse. Choose a goal. Close in. Conquer.'

Estelle smiled. 'Haven't you heard, Daddy? The journey is the destination.'

'Claptrap,' thundered Hed. 'Souvenir tea-towel slogans.'

But Estelle would not be drawn into argument. 'When I find what I'm looking for,' she told him, 'you'll be the first to know.' And with that she set off once more, leaving her father grumbling and cross and, frankly, very dangerous indeed.

Hed hated admitting he missed her, but his numerous card-playing cronies and business associates impatiently anticipated Estelle's return, for her presence had the effect of water sprinkled on hot coals. And Hed's quadrant of the universe was gaining a reputation for functioning far less peacefully in her absence.

24

It was hard enough keeping a small zoo healthy and solvent without having to worry about which animals could swim. It made Luke wonder whether the victims of all those big Biblical cataclysms had started out like this – with a sense of annoyance and doubt, a general conviction that they were merely going through a strange patch of weather, followed by slowly accelerating disbelief, followed by the terrible realization that they were all going to drown.

So far, the crisis had remained just this side of manageable, but last night they'd had frost. And yesterday's hail broke six windows in the café. Luke sighed. Having recorded drought, deluge, equatorial highs, freezing rain and hail, the Met Office had ceased to post predictions online. Phone calls jumped straight to a recorded message: *We are experiencing difficulties with our switchboard. Please call back later.*

Just this morning, all the managers had been called together to devise a series of emergency plans. They'd never had to worry about extra heating in June, and then just when they managed to get the system running, the temperature leapt thirty degrees in a single afternoon and everyone felt in danger of being roasted alive.

At least, Luke thought, the zoo was situated near the highest point of the city and, though subject to the same leaks and blocked drains as the rest of the population, had remained relatively dry.

Whenever he pictured animals up to their bellies and chins in water, Luke felt sick – so much so, that he found it hard to cope even with the thought of evacuation. How? Where to? Using what vehicles? How had Noah managed to pack rodents in with snakes and predatory birds? Could they expect penguins to waddle calmly up ramps into Land Rovers, like Labradors? Had anyone invented a floating horsebox for dromedaries? What about the caimans and crocodiles? He couldn't imagine any of it happening smoothly and besides, what would he use for staff? When his keepers failed to show up to work these days, it might be due to floods, melted tarmac, icy roads or any manner of surreal meteorological phenomena in between.

Luke lived on even higher ground than the zoo, at the top floor of a turn-of-the-century chateau-style apartment block with a green turret in one corner. He'd bought the flat because of the turret, which he used as his bedroom despite its draughty windows and curved walls. It was impossible to furnish, but in the end he settled for piles of books and a bed on the floor heaped with blankets, to compensate for the indoor weather.

No matter what frustrations his life threw up, the sweeping views from his room consoled him. Three great open vistas to east, south and west made him feel like the captain of a ship, navigating a vast landscape. He didn't even have to imagine the wind in his face. But now, for the first time, the outlook disturbed him. Reflections from vast puddles below filled his room with a strange flickery light. At night, the water made undulating patterns on his ceiling, like messages he couldn't interpret. Hail banging against his windows sounded eerie. When he dozed off for a few minutes, he dreamt of little pounding fists trying to get in.

His alarm clock glowed pale green in the dark: 3.25 a.m. Another sleepless night.

Local government offices issued repeated reassurances that the problem was under control. But when the mercury climbed past 47 degrees a state of emergency was called, and when it began to snow the newspapers ran headlines screaming APOCALYPSE NOW!

With a sigh, Luke got out of bed, pulled on a pair of jeans and went to stand at the window. The night was awful and beautiful, black and silver like an old photograph, its entire surface overlaid with grey streaks of rain. For a moment he longed for the particular – not the whole drowning world, but something personal: a partner in the foreground, putting everything else into perspective. A child.

He stood for a long time, watching the scene below. Neon signs fritzed on and off. Frozen fog softened the outlines of the landscape, transforming rectangles and squares into gentle lozenges and oblongs. Finally, at 4 a.m., with the half moon fizzing in the sky like an Alka-Seltzer tablet, he went back to bed.

25

By the time he was fully awake, the bell had been ringing for several minutes. At this time of the morning? He'd only just managed to fall asleep again.

'Hello.' The person at the door grinned. He had never laid eyes on her before. 'I'm your downstairs neighbour.'

Oh joy, thought Luke. 'How can I help you?' He barely managed to sound polite.

'I really hope you can? Aren't you going to, like, offer me a cup of tea?' The girl cocked her head. She couldn't have been more than sixteen, with the kind of smooth-featured face that looked even younger. 'You're not a morning person, are you? That's OK. I'll make the tea.'

Was he dreaming? The girl he'd never seen before was now in his kitchen making tea.

'Where do you keep the teabags?' And, when he pointed, 'I don't suppose you have soy?'

He stared at her. 'Sauce?'

'Milk. Never mind. I'll have mine, like, black? But you should really, like, try soy. I used to have all sorts of problems with things like, you know, bloat?'

She handed him a cup of tea. Despite all the chatter, he

was glad of it. 'My name's Skype? I bet you're, like, wondering why I'm here?'

'I don't mean to appear rude, but, yes. I am.' He glanced at his watch. Six fifteen. What sort of mad person goes around making friends at this hour?

She had found a seat at his table and he was awake enough, now, to look at her properly. She wore a T-shirt and hooded sweatshirt over a pleated school skirt; her broad smile revealed slightly uneven teeth.

'I need a, like, job?'

At this hour of the morning? He wondered at her inflections. Was she unsure about her need for a job? 'Do your parents know you're here? What about school?'

'I've only got one parent, actually, and I'm old enough to, like, come up here without telling my mum?' She grinned. 'School's nearly over. The thing is, you work at the zoo?'

He nodded. 'How do you happen to know that?'

She reached into her pocket and pulled out a brown envelope. 'Your payslip. It came to us by mistake?'

Luke's smile lacked enthusiasm. He reached for the envelope, wishing he could exchange this conversation for another ten minutes in bed.

'The thing is, I really need a job. And what with all the weather weirditude, I bet you need help?'

'Doing what, exactly?'

'I can do anything. Phones, admin, sweeping up. I could work for free for a while if you don't believe me?' For someone on the begging side of a non-existent job interview, Skype remained remarkably upbeat. 'And, by the way, this weather isn't going to last? I've done all the star charts and my friend Betts who's *UH-mazing* with predictions and stuff says another few weeks, max?'

Another few weeks? Great. Luke sighed. 'Let me think about it, if you don't mind. I'm not, as you said, much of a morning person. Besides, we haven't got the budget. Especially now.' He stood up, the universal signal (please, God) for dismissal.

Skype appeared unfazed. 'Great! I'll just finish my tea and be gone? *Begone! Forsooth!* Don't you love words like that? *Zounds!* Anyway, I can't stay cos I've got tai chi this morning? You ought to come, it would do you, like, so much good?'

Luke couldn't think of an appropriate response, but despite himself he smiled. Maybe he could find something for her to do. Wear a mouse costume and do a dance. Cheer up the troops.

She hovered by the door. 'I bet you thought I was, like, never going to leave? Mum says I'm like chewing gum on the bottom of a shoe.' She laughed. 'Don't forget, any job at all? Really, cos I'm desperate?'

He shut the door and finished his tea. He'd lived here three years and didn't know any of his neighbours, except by sight. A woman in her forties had recently moved in downstairs. Skype's mother? She'd looked fairly normal.

Luke pulled off his T-shirt and turned on the shower. They could probably use a bit of ticket-office cover for the people who couldn't get to work. What kind of a name was Skype, for Christ's sake? She was exactly the sort of kid who drove him mad, with her question-statements and her New Age soya milk. But enthusiasm was thin on the ground these days. Everyone was grumpy. Him, most of all.

26

Bob couldn't ever remember days passing this slowly. Mr B was buried in work, unwilling to engage in conversation – particularly on the subject of Lucy. The file Bob had accepted with bad grace this morning remained untouched. No way was he in any state to concentrate on Bumblebee Blight, *obviously*, what with not even liking bees, *or* honey, duh.

Bob kept shaking his watch, certain it had stopped, unable to accept that no time at all had passed since last he'd looked. At one point he actually watched the hands go from noon backwards to eleven, and if he'd been on speaking terms with Mr B he might have accused him of implementing one of his stupid lessons in forbearance.

Eventually it was time. He'd already changed outfits a dozen times, and without B's interference had settled upon narrow black jeans with a finely knitted T-shirt. It was too hot for anything else. At the last moment, he pulled on a pair of black Converse sneakers, grabbed an umbrella and told Eck not to leave the flat under any circumstances.

He felt awkward, worried that he'd chosen the wrong outfit to make a good impression on Lucy, but the truth was he didn't actually look bad. His face, when not screwed up in resentment, was not a bad face. He had fine cheekbones, a straight nose and clear skin, and at this moment his eyes (so often glazed over from too much sleep or self-abuse) looked bright with anticipation.

Eck watched him go without regret.

And then Bob was at the zoo, standing by the employees' gate. Waiting.

He had no idea what time Lucy actually finished work. Opening hours were listed on a sign at the entrance, and an hour or so after closing had seemed reasonable, but to be absolutely certain he'd arrived an hour before. Perhaps she worked till eight each night. How was he to know? Shouldn't Mr B have offered a briefing, composed a helpful call-sheet? Either would have been useful – or even a bit of last-minute advice. But no, always occupied with more important things, that was Mr B all over.

He felt hot. Wretched. Where was she? He checked his watch. He'd been standing around for nearly three hours. Did humans do this all the time? What a colossal waste of energy. Sex or no sex, he'd much rather be somewhere else. Submerged in a cool infinity pool off the coast of . . .

Just then, Lucy appeared in a flimsy dress printed with brightly coloured butterflies. Bob blinked. A cool breeze swept in from nowhere.

'Hello.' She looked away, blushing. She was shy, of course she was. Lovely Lucy, modest creature. Hardly more than a butterfly herself. Yes, he thought, delighted, she was a butterfly, a flitting creature, at once delicate and rare.

She laughed. 'Stop looking at me like that.'

'Like what?' His entire face had disappeared behind huge infatuated eyes.

'Like *that*,' she giggled. 'Like a crocodile contemplating lunch.' She took his arm. 'I'm glad you've got an umbrella. I lost mine at work yesterday and do you think anyone's turned it in? I wouldn't. This weather beggars belief, don't you think? It's boiling hot one minute and snowing the next.'

Her smile immobilized him. 'C-c-come,' was all he managed to stammer. 'Let's find something to eat.'

She knew a first-floor place nearby with air-conditioning. He'd have agreed to sky diving in the black hole of Calcutta as long as he could rest his hand on the curve of her waist forever.

The restaurant was crowded with people seeking refuge from the heat. Bob and Lucy waited, drinking ice water by a fan, till a couple got up to leave. While Bob was still looking around, captivated at finding himself in so human a place, Lucy greeted the waiter and ordered wine. She propped her chin up on two plump white hands. 'Hello,' she said, tilting her head happily to the left.

He gazed back at her, full of wonder. 'Hello.'

'What are you thinking?'

'I'm thinking how incredible it is that I managed to find you.'

'Amazing,' she smiled. 'I was thinking just the same.'

'You were?'

Her face was solemn. 'I was. I thought this job might turn out to be kind of lonely. Most of the visitors have kids, and most of the staff are either too old or too young. Or too ugly.' She grimaced and looked away, feeling a momentary pang about Luke, who was neither old nor ugly. Just mean.

'And then you turn up in the path of Izzy and me like you dropped off a cloud or something.'

'I'm the answer to your prayers.'

She laughed. 'I'll be the judge of that. Come on.' Her voice dropped suddenly, turning low, seductive. 'Tell me. What really brought you to the zoo?'

Bob hadn't prepared an answer to this question. He couldn't tell her how he scanned the planet day after day for girls, ending up in all sorts of strange places. Ashrams. Igloos. Zoos.

'I love animals,' Bob said, thinking mainly of mermaids. 'All animals, really.'

At that exact moment the statement was true. At that exact moment, staring at the beautiful arc of Lucy's cheekbone, with the warmth of her smile radiating across the table towards him, his pride and passion for all the creatures he'd created threatened to overwhelm him. A tear came to his eye for all the good he'd done, all the wonders he could claim credit for. Tonight, the world was a perfect place. Sitting close to Lucy in the tiny restaurant, cooled by the fans while moonlight slid silently across the windows, he couldn't think of a single way to improve it. Too much heat, maybe. Outside, the temperature plunged. He gazed at Lucy, who gazed back at him.

'I sensed you loved animals. But you'd better fill in the rest. I don't know anything at all about you, not even your last name.'

He looked down. 'You couldn't possibly be interested.'

'But I am.' She sat back. 'Go on.'

'OK, then. Let's see.' Bob took a deep breath. 'I come from a galaxy about four hundred million light years away, and came here ages ago when the job of supreme godhead was unexpectedly offered to me. Then I created everything, heaven and earth, beasts of the field, creatures of the sea and sky, etc., and one day while hanging around I saw your prayer and it all led up to me sitting here tonight with you.'

'Nice story,' laughed Lucy.

Bob shrugged. Unsmiling, he lowered his hand next to her elbow, settling his forearm gently beside a pool of tomato sauce and oily mozzarella. 'Everything in my life has led me to this moment, sitting beside you. So tell me all about *you*.'

'No, it's not good enough. What do you do? Where are you from? Seriously, this time. Your accent, for starters . . . I can't place it.' She folded her arms. 'Go on, start from the beginning.'

'The beginning?'

'Yup. "I was born . . . I grew up . . ."'

'I was born in . . . I grew up . . .' His eyes skittered to the corners of the room. 'We travelled all over the place when I was little. I learned lots of languages. That's why you can't place me.'

'Ha! I thought so. You don't sound like anyone I've met before. So – Africa? Asia? America? Was your father in the navy or something?'

Bob looked away. 'Something like that.'

'Much more interesting than my family. My dad's a solicitor, defends people with tax havens. Mum wears blouses with bows and helps my godfather out at the church. Very sensible.' She giggled.

An image of Mona floated uninvited into Bob's head. 'She sounds great, actually. My mother's a fruitcake.'

'Really?' Lucy looked worried. 'So, not really cut out to be a navy wife?'

Bob shook his head mournfully. 'She ran off. Soon after I was born.' This much, at least, was true.

Lucy reached for his arm. 'Poor you. You probably don't trust women an inch.' She wasn't entirely sure what to make of his family history, but nonetheless sensed something vulnerable in Bob, something lonely and worthy of love. Her fingers closed over his.

Bob kissed her and the room began to crackle and hum with sheet lightning. A bottle slid off the table. The electrical disturbance lasted only a few seconds, for the duration of the kiss. Lucy pulled back, a little dazed, hands trembling, eyes darting around the room. When she collected herself, she took in the broken glass, the stack of menus now splayed across the floor. The restaurant owner gripped on to the edge of the bar as if uncertain whether to trust his chair.

'What was that?' Lucy's eyes were wide.

'What?' He could still feel her mouth on his.

'*What?* You must have felt it.' She glanced at the other diners to confirm what she'd seen. Nervous laughter had lasted only a moment, and normal conversation was returning slowly.

Bob didn't seem to hear. He couldn't take his eyes off her. 'It might have been the foundations of the building settling . . . you know, all this water?'

Lucy nodded, frowning a little, and he pressed the entire bundle of her fingers to his lips. 'Lucy, I . . .' He could barely speak. 'You're so beautiful.' He disengaged one hand and touched her cheek with his fingers. 'So perfect. Such a perfect,

perfect girl.' Any words he might once have planned deserted him. He realized with a jolt that Lucy was *his* creation. How had he managed to make a creature so elegant, so eloquent, so full of empathy? And so willing to love him? He gazed at her with wonder, humble wonder for the existence of this girl. None of his powers allowed him to make sense of what he felt.

Tears filled his eyes and he had to turn away. The aloneness of his life up until this moment made him gasp. He thought of a boy, impaled through the gut on the uprights of a metal railing, gasping his last gasps of life. That's how he had always felt. Run through with loneliness.

Her glass was nearly empty and he tipped the last of the wine into it, his hand unsteady with emotion.

'Careful,' she smiled. 'You'll have to carry me home.'

'I would do that gladly.' He could almost feel her soft weight in his arms.

'You'd do yourself an injury,' she giggled.

Time passed and the hour grew late. The waiter settled quietly at a corner table with his accounts. They were the only customers left, talking softly together.

'I never thought I'd meet anyone in my job either,' Bob whispered.

'What is your job?'

'Oh, you know.' He looked away. 'Just one of those jobs. Executive consultancy sort of thing. Too boring to go into.'

'Aren't you a bit –' she frowned – 'young, to be a consultant?'

Bob shrugged. 'You know how it goes. Right time, right place.'

Business prodigy or family connections, Lucy thought.

Bob met her eyes. 'I don't want to talk about work. I want

to talk about you.' He leaned in close and whispered. 'Tell me a secret.'

'Me?' She laughed. 'I haven't got one.' And then, lowering her voice, expression grave, she said, 'I let one of the capybaras escape. I still haven't found him.'

Bob frowned. 'Capybara?'

'They're a kind of giant rodent. Like a guinea pig crossed with a hippo.' She looked mournful. 'Skinny little legs. Bristly hair. They're actually quite sweet.'

He vaguely remembered creating something of that description, but couldn't remember why. 'Will you be in trouble?'

Lucy giggled and cupped her hand round his ear. 'I could lose my job. But so far no one's noticed.'

Her warm breath aroused him. He turned his head to kiss her. 'Never mind about the job. I'll take care of you.'

They sat like that for a long time and Lucy tipped over into a state of perfect happiness. This is what it's like, she thought. This is how love feels, as if we're the only two people in the world, perfectly attuned, hiding together, united against the elements while the whole world hovers. I will never, ever forget this moment.

He kissed the crease of her elbow, closing it over his mouth.

Outside, the night was soft and crystal clear. It had turned cold. Men and women wearing flimsy clothing hurried home through the streets, shivering and hugging themselves. Seen through the large front window of the restaurant, the sky glowed with the cold white light of stars. A few flakes of snow fell. The waiter threw open the windows and turned off the air-conditioner.

Lucy gasped. 'It's happening again, look!' The sky was

filled with shooting stars. Bob sat back, smiling, while Lucy and the waiter leaned out and laughed like children. 'What a night. What a strange day, and series of days, but what a wonderful glorious night. If the world were to end tonight, I wouldn't complain a bit.' Her voice trailed off.

The waiter refused to charge them for the meal. Not on a night like this, he said. Bob and Lucy turned away from each other, shy to have been witnessed, and grateful too. Out on the street, Lucy shivered and Bob put his arm round her shoulders.

'It's heaven being cold. But strange.'

'Come on, let's find your rodent,' said Bob.

She looked at him. 'You'd help me? But he could be anywhere.'

Bob shrugged. 'Can't hurt to look. Come on,' he said, 'we'll try. We'll imagine ourselves lost capybaras and think where we'd go.'

'We'll never find him. They can swim like rats. And love to lie underwater with only their noses sticking out.'

'OK, we'll find a boat and search for noses.'

Lucy beamed. 'Really? You're, you're . . .'

'A god among men?'

'Yes.' She laughed.

'And you – are a goddess among women.' He did not smile. It was too important.

He found a boat, just where one should have been.

'How do you do that?' she asked.

He shrugged again, helped her climb aboard and pushed off.

'I'm a water nymph,' she said, trailing one hand over the side of the rowboat, drunk with wine and admiration.

They rowed through the entire flooded area below the zoo, peering into every little copse and shed, increasingly aware of the hopelessness of their mission. After an hour or so, every bobbing plastic bottle took the shape of a rogue snout, and the zig-zagging sweeps of the little boat turned ever more hilarious.

'Let's stop,' Lucy said at last, choking with laughter after spending ten minutes chasing a plastic beer keg. 'He could be anywhere. It's impossible.'

It wasn't far to Lucy's house.

Bob tied up the boat and they clambered over on to her balcony, standing silent in front of the French doors, watching the sparkle of moonlight on water. Boats glided quietly past; they caught the occasional murmur of a far-off conversation. At the end of the road, a couple drifted by playing a strange duet on violin and penny whistle. Bob kissed her lips, felt the blood pulse warm in her, willing the moment to go on and on. They kissed again, trembling with the hesitance of disbelief. It was a kiss as pure as the first kiss in the history of the world. Behind them more stars fell from the sky.

They kissed again, and then again, until Lucy at last pulled back while Bob hovered, anguished, incandescent, willing her to invite him in. For a moment she appeared to be bracing herself against a fierce wind, her expression woozy, her bones soft. But then she stiffened and gently pushed him away.

'Not yet,' she whispered, her expression soft and blurry with desire.

'I love you,' he whispered back.

Lucy closed her eyes and breathed deeply, inhaling the air

that contained his words. She needed to make it last, to extend desire, the wanting and not having, until the irresistible pull became stronger than any force on Earth. And then, she thought, we'll come together and experience a consummation of love that will shimmer forever, as long as we both shall live.

Bob shared Lucy's passion, but his plans were more short-term.

He wasn't thinking of forever, of growing old with Lucy as his wife, sitting together on a bench in some windswept seaside town, her elderly swollen ankles in stout black shoes, distended knuckles resting on arthritic knees. Such visions meant nothing to him because he would always be exactly as he was now, despite the passage of time. His humans would change, grow old and die, disappear from Earth and be forgotten, while he went on the same.

For this reason, it was the present that interested him, even in the deepest sincerest most passionate throes of love. Lucy now, not Lucy later. Of course he might have concluded the issue in a variety of non-legitimate ways, disappearing and reappearing in Lucy's bedroom, making a slight alteration in the arrangement of time and space. But even Bob had the wit to recognize that no matter how it's framed, rape is still rape – which besides falling morally short of suitable (as Mr B had explained to him, time and again) took most of the pleasure out of conquest. Besides, he loved her. And he wasn't totally devoid of self-control. He could wait until next time, holding her image in his head. He didn't want to wait, obviously, but he would.

He sighed and met her eyes. 'Hey.'

'Hey, yourself. I really should go . . .' She smiled. 'Give me your number and I'll text you tomorrow.'

He shifted a little, looked away.

'Where's your phone?' She'd pulled hers out, ready to record his number.

'I don't carry one.'

'Landline, then.'

He shook his head.

She stared at him. 'You're living with someone.'

'I am *not*.' He dipped his head, looking up at her through his fringe, like a pony. 'I just don't . . . like . . . phones.'

'Really.' She felt sick.

'Really! Truly.'

Lucy frowned at him, doubtful, wanting to believe. 'Wow,' she said at last. 'I thought everyone had a phone.'

'I guess they do. But I'm not really like everyone . . .'

'I think I noticed that.' Staring at him, hands on hips, she looked suddenly formidable. 'Swear to God you're not living with someone?'

What the hell. 'Swear. Do I look married?'

She hesitated. 'No. You don't look married.'

He held out his palms to her and slowly she gave him her hands. They were cold.

'Where do you live?'

He has never shared this information. It is not as if he has had to register for tax, or have a newspaper delivered. Besides, his abode is, you might say, unfixed – in that he and Mr B have a tendency to move around quite a bit. As whim and necessity require it.

When he looks up, Lucy is squinting at him. He can feel

the importance of the moment. He exhales and says the address quickly, and she repeats it to herself, *number twelve*, mouthing the words slightly. She nods, as if this is all she requires to believe that he is real.

Her shoulders dropped a fraction. 'OK, so, carrier pigeons, then?' There was still doubt in her voice, but he observed with joy that the crisis had passed.

'I'll have to find you in person. You can see the advantage.'

He kissed her again. Slightly dazed, Lucy opened the door, hesitated, then pulled it shut behind her. He didn't go, but stood gazing at her through the glass, while she watched the sky behind him, criss-crossed with trails of light.

What a girl, thought Bob. What a girl.

'She's just a garden-variety God-bothering professional virgin,' Mr B said, without looking up. 'Please take your boots off in the house. And if you don't mind, I'd appreciate a transfer of attention from your loins to the worldwide meteorological situation.' Peering through his spectacles he indicated the window, where water was now threatening to slosh over the windowsills. The respite had passed, and once again it was raining. 'It's past a joke.'

Bob scowled. 'It's all my fault, is that what you're saying?'

'Yes, that's precisely what I'm saying. And if you'd be so good as to stop sulking, we might achieve some degree of improvement. Really, now, what could be simpler?'

'You don't understand, do you? You *know* I can't just turn it off.'

'But you could try, surely?' He always managed to put on a pleasant face, despite the ache in *his* heart.

'I *am* trying.'

Very trying, thought Mr B.

In the middle of the Pacific, tsunamis gained momentum. Tornadoes devastated Kansas and the eastern Chinese coastal province of Jiangsu. An upside-down rainbow had been spotted over Sicily. News updates reported snow falling on the Sahara desert. While right here at home, the temperature raced up and down between boiling and freezing and stars fell out of the sky more or less at random.

And all because the Almighty had fallen head over heels in love with an assistant zookeeper. It wasn't a joke, and would become less of a joke as the situation progressed. God falls in love; thousands die. Mr B couldn't, in all conscience, leave Earth in such a state.

'Here,' he said, handing a file to Bob. 'Some helpful hints on weather catastrophes around the world, and how to prevent them. If at all possible. If you would be so kind.'

Bob snatched the file and stomped out without a word. But what about me, he thought. What about the fact that I'm in love? Doesn't that matter more than these stupid jobs?

Two hours later, Mr B leaned back in his chair, yawned and rubbed his eyes. The familiar throbbing ache had emerged above his left temple. Outside, occasional rumbles of thunder punctuated the steady drizzle.

Mr B's plan went along the lines of whisking his charge away to safety in a haze of smoochy bliss – after which the rain would stop and life would return to normal in time for him to wave goodbye to Bob and his miserable planet without a backwards glance. Of course it wouldn't solve the problem for good. Life would only remain stable till the next drop-dead gorgeous waitress/tree surgeon/dog-walker caught Bob's eye. But by then it would no longer be his problem.

Thinking of Bob's previous failed relationships, Mr B succumbed to a deep resignation. As the unwilling puppet master, he would tug gently on each string, controlling the movement of one foot, then another, pulling an arm back from a fondle that could endanger them both. He might cause a head to nod and a shoulder to shrug, but while he was concentrating on this, a sweaty hand might creep forward of its own volition to caress a tender length of thigh.

And which one of them, on which end of the strings, could be considered less free?

27

Eck had determined to enjoy the last few weeks of his life, but was finding it increasingly difficult. Bob spent most of his time mooning over Lucy and Mr B worked all the time, so there was no one to nudge and joggle him out of his low spirits. In the past, he and Bob might play computer games together or watch a film; they'd had tournaments to see who could balance the most dinner plates on one finger or eat the most cake. Sometimes Bob showed him pictures of naked girls and asked which he liked best, but Eck couldn't choose. He found short noses unattractive.

Time seemed to be passing so quickly.

On this day, he woke from a depressed doze to see Estelle waving at him through the window. At first his heart leapt to see her, but on second thoughts he approached with some trepidation. It was this girl's father, after all, who planned to eat him. Perhaps her show of friendliness was merely a ruse. Perhaps her father had sent Estelle to nibble him first, to make sure sadness hadn't made him bitter.

But could the expression of kindness on her face be false? She held out her arms to him. 'You seem thinner,' she said, frowning.

Despite being quite a suspicious Eck, he found it impossible to deny the inherent appeal of Estelle's face, particularly in comparison with the other faces he knew. She didn't smile at him in a threatening way, or a way that suggested she wanted something, or was just barely managing not to laugh at him. She smiled in a way that made him feel as if he were the creature she most wanted to see in the whole entire world.

No one had ever looked at Eck in quite this way, and he was so moved by the experience that he forgot his suspicions and shuffled forward into her arms. He remembered how she had held him on the night of the terrible game, and screwed his eyes shut to erase the rest of the memory. He hadn't known it was possible to experience so many intense feelings at once – misery, love, hunger, suspicion, excitement and of course the ever-present terror of mortality. The enormity of it made him quiver like a leaf.

He lay still, eyes closed, while she explained about her absence and her travels, the places she'd been and the creatures she'd met, and then she stroked and tickled him, and spoke to him in her singy voice. It was only much later that she gently disengaged herself and reached for her large leather bag.

The Eck scrambled up, eyes wide with alarm. Estelle's bag looked exactly like the sort of thing you threw over the head of a man about to be hanged.

'Here,' she said, and handed it to him. 'I brought you some things.'

Trembling with dread, Eck peered into the horrible bag. On top was a cake and beside it a long sandwich stuffed with roast beef, pickles, tomatoes and cheese.

Throughout his life, the Eck had dreamt constantly of being full – full of happiness, praise or kindness, yes – but most persistently, full of food. And now here, on this most inauspicious of days, Estelle appeared and offered as much sandwich as he could eat, followed by three cakes of perfect deliciousness, fresh scones with jam from a planet that specialized only in jam, a jar of celestial gherkins, pancakes rolled with exquisite condiments unknown in the Milky Way, fruit pies, and the sort of rich, creamy cheese Eck imagined one might eat in heaven. Even if the purpose of the snack was to fatten him up for the kill, it was still extremely nice.

'Bob's not here?'

Eck shook his head. He was unable to tell whether she was pleased or disappointed, for her expression remained neutral.

Conversation did not flow at first. Eck's mouth was not designed to hold more than half a sandwich and it currently held three. His greed amused the girl, who offered him delicacy after delicacy. The sheer volume of food caused his cheeks to bulge and his eyes to roll back in his head. And all the time he ate, she told him tales of things he had never even thought to imagine. The sound of her voice thrilled him almost as much as the stories and, despite the depressing facts of his fate, he felt almost happy.

'I'm sorry I haven't been to see you,' said the girl.

The Eck nodded.

'Now I'm back,' she said. 'And do you know why?'

Eck examined the question from every angle. It seemed a bit risky to guess.

Estelle looked at him, her expression steady. 'It's because

I like you. And also because I'm extremely unhappy about my father's bet.'

Not as unhappy as I am, thought Eck.

'I . . .' She paused to select precisely the right words. 'I am doing what I can to influence him. But in the meantime, I should like us to be friends.'

Eck nodded, a bit uncertainly. He supposed that in the absence of a future, a friend might be nice.

'Shall we go outside?'

Eck drooped.

'It's all right – you're allowed.' She looked up and saw Mr B watching them from the doorway. 'Hello,' she said. 'We're going out for some air. Would you like to join us?'

Yes, he would like to join them. The thought of passing a few hours drifting about in the company of Estelle was irresistible. But there was work to do. Always. Too much work. An infinity of work. So he declined, politely, with regret.

As they went out, Estelle turned back to face Mr B. 'Next time,' she said.

It sounded more like a plan than a query.

She took Eck to the zoo, and despite the rain they spent a happy afternoon in the company of the penguins, who fascinated Eck the way monkeys fascinate small children. So similar and yet so different.

When a keeper came past with a bucket of fish, Eck hid behind Estelle, though the keeper-girl didn't look as if she were noticing much of anything beside her own thoughts.

'Eck,' Eck whispered to Estelle, and Estelle nodded. So, this was the girl Bob had fallen for. The nice girl from the café. What a shame. And what a small world Earth was, she thought, relieved that Lucy was too distracted to notice them. She doubted her description of Eck's provenance would stand up to scrutiny a second time.

When it came time to drop Eck off at home, the girl waylaid a possible bout of weeping by producing a slightly shop-worn pork chop from her coat pocket. Eck stretched his snout in its direction.

'Do help yourself,' she said.

The creature helped himself. 'Eck,' he mumbled, and she saw big mingled tears of joy and sadness well up in his eyes. Long watery trails ran down to his chin.

Estelle placed a reassuring hand on his shoulder. She would have loved to tell him not to worry, that it would all turn out fine, but she couldn't be confident that it would. Her father was a particularly tricky individual. And she, it must be said, was distracted by her quest . . . for heaven knew what.

Eck shook his head and snuffled her hands and arms; then with some deference, and when she seemed not to object, he licked her carefully with his long sticky tongue. She tasted of fresh limes and rainwater.

'Shall we meet again tomorrow?' She watched him with her head tilted slightly to one side, her eyes simultaneously cool and warm.

Eck shook his head gloomily. Bob would be home any minute. He would never allow Eck to have a friend.

'Next day?' she said.

The creature brightened. Perhaps Bob would have disappeared by the next day. Perhaps by the next day, the world as he knew it would have changed into something else.

Everything might have altered, as it seemed to do with disconcerting frequency these days.

'OK, then, next day,' said the girl, and waved goodbye.

A friend, thought Eck. Of course she probably wanted something from him, but he didn't mind. He couldn't afford to be selective about friends, having had no other offers, and none likely in the foreseeable future. After which he would be dead.

Mr B stood at the window and watched her disappear into the drizzle. His brow was as creased as ever, but his eyes, uncharacteristically, shone.

28

'Who is that girl?' Mr B asked Bob.

'Which girl?'

'The one Eck's taken a shine to.'

'Oh, her. Miss Plainy-Pants. Her father's that scary Mafioso guy. The one who's going to –' They both looked at Eck, who stood defiantly in the corner of the room, staring into the middle distance. 'You know.'

Mr B nodded.

Only in the afternoons, when Estelle came to see him, did Eck perk up at all. The strain of living under a sentence of death bled his spirit.

They ate in silence. Eck had stopped begging at the table for scraps; even his insatiable hunger seemed to have waned. Hunger was just another pain he endured now as evidence that he was still alive – along with despair. If he starved, well, maybe it wasn't the worst way to die.

'And she's the daughter?'

'Who?'

'Miss Plainy-Pants.'

Bob shrugged. 'Eloise. Esmerelda. Weaselly thing.'

Mr B dissented silently. Not weaselly. With her long straight nose, pale skin and high forehead, the girl might have walked straight out of an early Renaissance painting. Not at all weaselly. She was slim and graceful; she moved without flapping or fuss.

Returning to work, Mr B flipped through his files of pleading humans, page after page, avoiding their eyes, trying to answer their prayers, his brain flitting back to . . . Esmerelda?

One file slithered out, an Indian child with serious brown eyes and a depth and complexity of expression. He had rabies, and the petition came from his father. Mr B stared down at the child's face for some time. Untreated, he knew, the boy would develop a vast, unquenchable thirst as his throat and jaw muscles grew rigid with paralysis. Death would follow in a matter of hours.

Mr B rubbed his head. It wasn't that he didn't like to fix things. But every adjustment led to unexpected repercussions, a chain of reactions certain to render the original deed null and void. He'd had plenty of experiences like that: the sweet child saved from death, who grew up to be Vlad the Impaler.

Mr B felt like some sort of cursed accountant, with figures that eternally refused to add up.

But sometimes he had no choice. For himself, as much as for anyone. This time, just the slightest nudge, a tap, almost. Enough so that a visiting doctor from a UN special task force might slip over sideways, a mile or two off his intended path. Enough to cross paths with the boy's father.

Of course these operations took time, were as technical as the isolation of a single grain of sand on an infinite stretch of beach. And who knew what else the nudge displaced? The tap that slipped the doctor sideways could slide a lorry into a crowd, topple a climber into a ravine, nudge a surgeon's blade. And for what? To postpone a single incident of death or suffering because one face in ten billion had caught his eye?

Was he the only one who found this situation intolerable?

Moving the Indian boy's file caused the whales to slither out of the heap and on to the floor at his feet. In his head, Mr B heard their desperate voices. Thirty-metre baleen whales had been sighted in unfeasibly warm seas, searching for krill that were searching for phytoplankton. Others turned up gasping on beaches, their sonar confused by hunger and illness and noise. The tiniest ecological shift had already begun to make life impossible for them, thanks to an elegant anomaly in their biology – for Mr B, a far more accomplished creator than Bob, had devised a food chain with just two short links. Plankton to whale. So beautifully simple. Until something went wrong with the plankton.

The whales did not plead with sad looks or sagging shoulders. Their huge, impassive faces expressed nothing but the eternal stoicism of their race. Mr B could face them in a way that he could not face the humans, who were, after all, created in the image of Bob, complete with all Bob's tragic flaws and an infinite chocolate-box selection of tragic outcomes.

He couldn't bear the thought of those plangent voices being silenced forever, but he knew that they would soon cease to ask for help, having despaired of it coming. He bent down slowly, with a grunt, and lifted the file up on to his desk.

I will help you, he said silently to the whales. For my own sake as well as for yours, I will help you.

He wondered that the cetaceans had remained loyal to him, that they knew they were different. They were the only species with the intelligence to contact him directly, bypassing not only human intervention, but also Bob, for they (quite sensibly) did not believe in him.

Their keen brains and their beauty touched him almost as deeply as their faith in his power to save them. He could not leave without knowing that his own creations (at the very least) had been saved from painful oblivion.

His thoughts strayed once more to Eck's friend, as he jotted down a message, for immediate delivery.

I will help you.

29

Accompanied by the shuffling feet and muffled snorts of wild boars and oryx, Lucy swept water from the corridor with a wide brush. It was the perfect occupation; anything requiring more concentration would have been impossible.

Outside, the rain came down in vengeful sheets, slamming against the metal roof with a violence that suited her state of mind. Emotional overdrive had rendered her fantasies almost hallucinogenic: those lips, the slender fingers, the deeply shadowed, troubled eyes.

She felt skinless. Every thought in her head was of him.

CRR . . . *AACK*! Thunder seemed to emanate from inside the building, inside her head. She pressed both hands over her ears to shut it out.

Who could she talk to? Who would understand? Her body no longer seemed to belong to her; she was flotsam caught in a howling whirlpool . . . and Bob, Bob was the force.

'Sleeping on the job?'

She jerked up, began sweeping the water again, vigorously. Luke. Of course. 'Nearly finished here. Just stopped to catch my breath.' She couldn't keep the edge out of her voice.

He looked at her. 'No rush. Just checking to see if you needed help.'

Right. 'Thanks. I'm fine.'

CRRR . . . *ACK!*

'Christ!' he said. 'That was a bit close.'

She felt wary of him, and frightened. The way he looked at her was so critical. Did he suspect about the capybara, or was he just keeping an eye on her, watching for a slip-up?

Water had begun to run down the inside of one wall and Luke swore, then hesitated for a moment as if about to say something else.

Lucy steeled herself, but when she looked again there was something in his expression that stopped her. His face was neither critical nor contemptuous. More . . . puzzled. Concerned. And then he smiled at her, actually smiled, and she nearly looked over her shoulder because it seemed so unlikely. But before she could clarify the odd encounter he was gone, and she shook him out of her head. There was barely room for him in it anyway.

She needed to see Bob again, needed his arms round her to stop the buzzing anxiety in her blood. What spell had he cast? Nothing existed in her life except his face, his hands, his eyes. Need tugged at her like the pull of the moon on the sea, exerting a force so great she thought she might die of it.

And then he was beside her.

She gasped. 'Oh, Bob. I was just . . .'

'Shhh.' He put a finger to her lips, took her hands in his and kissed her mouth and eyes, burying his face in her hair.

'My God,' she sighed, face flushed, eyes half-shut.

Yes, he thought.

She clung to him.

'I want to be with you. Properly,' he murmured, and she nodded. Her compliance thrilled him.

They couldn't stay here. He kissed her again, delighted by the feel and the smell and the taste of her. 'Lucy,' he said. 'My darling. Can you meet me tonight? Now?'

'I . . .' She hesitated. 'We've all volunteered to work late tonight. I'm not sure I can get out of it.'

He frowned. 'Well, what if I came with you? I can help too.' They could work side by side, almost like equals, and then afterwards . . .

She looked doubtful. 'Are you sure?'

'Of course.' He set his face in an expression of confidence that faded to something uneasy. 'Will I know what to do?'

She laughed. 'Of course.' Lucy imagined them working together, showing him off to her workmates. 'You'll be fine. It'll be really useful to have another pair of hands.'

'OK, then, let's do it.' He kissed her again.

'Two minutes,' she gasped, and pointed him in the direction of the staff offices.

Inside the low building, it felt crowded and humid. Sheet lightning illuminated the room at erratic intervals. Bob wrinkled his nose. Humans smelled stronger than he remembered.

Lucy was the last to arrive. She slipped her arm through Bob's, took a deep breath and led him over to the group by the coffee machine, feeling unaccountably embarrassed when Luke introduced himself and offered his hand. Bob took hold of it, grasping it loosely at arm's length without moving. To her mortification, he seemed to have forgotten how a handshake worked. Luke blinked, and withdrew carefully. He caught Lucy's eye.

She looked away, blushing.

Well, well, well, thought Luke. What a strange one he is. If he were a dog, I'd give him a wide berth.

All the hay, straw and sawdust bedding had to be restacked on to piles of wooden pallets. Rain had already seeped through the corrugated iron roof and pooled on the floor. There were twelve volunteers in six teams of two. Lucy and Bob held hands, staking out their partnership, which left four others, including Luke, who paired up with the new girl from the ticket office.

Where on earth had Luke found her, Lucy wondered, checking out the girl's vegan neo-hippy-eco-ethnic dress sense. Her black hair was cut short, with a single skinny plait down the back, and Lucy noticed that she treated Luke with easy familiarity, which was impressive. Even the staff who liked him kept a bit of a distance. Maybe she has lots of brothers, thought Lucy, trying to eavesdrop on the girl's stream of babble.

'I should be at home,' Skype was saying, 'like, revising? Which is, like, bullshit, obviously, when the world is, like, coming to an end?'

'That's not what you said last time. A few more weeks of bad weather, wasn't it?' Luke was all reproach.

'A few weeks?' She shrugged. 'Or a few million years? Who knows?'

Luke again caught Lucy's eye, this time with a little

half-smile. Once more, the intimacy of the glance shook her.

'C'mon, Luke, let's go.' Skype was tugging on his sleeve now. 'Our team's on, like, hay bales?'

He smiled, to himself this time, and followed her.

The bales were heavy and awkward to lift and it was exhausting work, but Bob and Lucy toiled stoically for the first half hour. To her surprise, Lucy discovered that she possessed more strength and stamina than her partner, for Bob began to flag well before tea break. Jollying him along with kisses and encouragement, Lucy found herself unaccountably irritated by the sound of Luke and Skype laughing as they worked. He seemed to enjoy having an adoring girl in tow. And what kind of stupid name was Skype, anyway?

At tea break, Lucy fetched two cups, returning to find Skype hunkered down on a bale talking to Bob. The combination made her flinch.

'So, like, I didn't have a job, and I went up to Luke and I was, like, OK, so why don't you give me one? A job, I mean? And he did?'

Bob looked nonplussed.

Skype leaned in. 'Don't you think this is all just so *UH-mazing*? You know what I mean?'

Bob didn't. He took a nervous step backwards.

'Like the weather and all of us working together to, like, save the animals? I feel like Noah with the flood.' Skype leapt to her feet and climbed nimbly to the top of the bales, suddenly raising her voice and punching the air for emphasis. 'And God said, *BEHOLD*, I shall bring a flood of water upon the land, to destroy all flesh and *EVERYTHING*

SHALL PERISH!' She lowered her arms. 'What a miserable old shit God must be.'

Eyes huge, Bob cast about desperately for Lucy, who had just arrived with the tea and a packet of biscuits.

Skype gave a little wave and scarpered back off to Luke.

'What was that about?' Lucy asked.

Bob stood unnaturally rigid.

'Sorry I couldn't save you.' Lucy handed Bob his cup of tea. 'Only another half hour, and then we'll go.' She'd had enough, more than enough. The sexy feeling of working beside Bob had worn off, leaving her tired and depressed. The rain had stopped briefly, but a rumbling thunderstorm seemed to be building again from some distance away. Through the high windows, lightning continued to flash.

'It's really tragic, all this peculiar weather,' Lucy said as they left the zoo together. She stopped to stare at a ruined pushchair, overturned in a puddle. 'So many lives messed up.' They walked in silence for a moment. 'I heard on the news that the death toll is in the thousands.'

Bob shoved his hands in his pockets and looked away. 'It's not my fault,' he muttered.

Lucy laughed a little quizzically and took his arm. 'Of course it's not.'

But Bob fidgeted, disgruntled and obscurely guilty, and she had to push the hair out of his eyes, make faces at him, tangle her feet in his, and nearly trip him up in the knee-deep water. What happened to the other Bob? she wondered. The one who can't keep his hands off me?

'Let's go home,' Lucy whispered in his ear, nuzzling his

neck, and at last he broke off from his conundrums and complexities of thought. She drew her jacket tight, wishing Bob would put his arms round her. He was in his shirtsleeves. 'Aren't you cold?'

But he wasn't. 'I don't feel the cold,' he said, which was perfectly true.

They walked and walked. Great forks of lightning flashed on all sides; thunder crashed overhead. But the sky was clear, and no rain fell.

Bob seemed out of sorts and finally Lucy could take no more. She hauled him into a doorway and kissed him passionately, and at last he seemed to notice her. They kissed again; Bob wound her hair round his fingers and stroked her face. 'That's better,' she murmured, her head pressed into the crease of his neck.

At her house, she fumbled with the door, and then they were inside, still kissing. Taking her face in his hands, he lifted the hair off her neck and dipped his head to kiss the exposed skin of her shoulder. Her skin tasted tangy and sweet. He took her arms and wrapped them round his waist, holding them there, nuzzling deep into the softness below her jawbone, kissing her ear, her eyelid, the corner of her mouth. She felt herself being drawn deeper and deeper into a dark place, spinning beyond time.

Another crash. Panic rose suddenly in Lucy, displacing passion. *What?* she thought wildly. *What's happening?* Wrenching free, she caught sight of herself in the mirror and stopped, startled. The girl staring back at her had hair that hung loose in tangled pale ropes, burning cheeks, huge dilated pupils, bruised lips. She was wild with wanting, wild with fear, beyond control. Is that me? she wondered. Is that *me*?

Flash! Crash!

Panting, she turned to Bob and stared in wonder at the light flowing round his outline – dripping from his fingertips, his eyes, as if he were too full of light to contain it.

Lucy shivered and hugged herself. Who *is* he?

Blinking with confusion, she retreated to the kitchen. 'Cup of tea?'

'Tea?' The light around him flickered and died. Bob stared.

'I have chamomile and builder's.' She tried to smile from behind the breakfast bar, but it was misery she felt. Misery, confusion and fear.

'No.' He ducked round the edge of the worktop to her and, frowning slightly, put his hands on her shoulders.

She spun away. 'I'll just put the kettle on. If you don't mind.'

He looked on with a pained expression as she filled the kettle, checked her answerphone, stacked the mail neatly in a wooden box beside the toaster. He wanted to scream when she pulled out a sponge and began scrubbing at a spot of jam on the laminate worktop. And then she stopped.

'Bob,' she said carefully, not daring to look at him, 'I think you'd better go.'

He came to her once more and pulled her close, earnest with need, but she slipped out of his arms. 'Please. If we start again, I won't be able to stop. I need . . .' What did she need? Someone who wasn't Bob? 'I need . . . more time. A lot more time.'

'Well, bravo for her, I say.' Mr B looked genuinely cheered.

'A bit unnatural, though, don't you think, darling?' Mona

frowned. Then brightened. 'Still, it's helpful.' She consulted her list, which had begun to look battered. She hadn't yet succeeded in making Bob a better God . . . or fixing the weather . . . and as for Lucy . . .

Mona sighed, and disappeared.

Mr B fervently hoped Bob's courtship of Lucy would be successful. It seemed the only way to adjust the world's meteorological problems without entering Bob's Wonderful World of Sexual Dismay too quickly. The hour of hazy sunshine this afternoon had encouraged him. A few much-needed rainclouds had even materialized over central Africa. But the thunder was disturbing.

'I'd say the girl is obviously quite gaga over you.' He spoke cautiously.

Bob looked gloomily at the floor. 'I love her more than the moon and the stars. And all that stuff.'

'Of course.' Mr B paused, wondering how much Bob cared for the moon and the stars, if at all. 'Well, clever old you. She's obviously a girl worth having.'

'You don't even have the first idea. She's amazing. She's miraculous. She's the most incredible, beautiful girl. And *I* made her.'

Mr B raised an eyebrow.

Bob recoiled. 'Not like *that*. I made the people who made her and the ones who made them and the ones who made them. And so on and so on, back and back and back. And each set of perfect combinations came together because of the way *I* made them.'

'You *are* a genius.'

'I am.'

'And your decision to move slowly is an excellent one . . .'

Bob's laughter was scornful. 'You're giving *me* advice on how to seduce a woman? You? Mr Useless Old Past-It with bells on?'

What a wit the boy had. What a keen knife's edge of irony. What a bloody prodigy he was, oh, yes indeed, a definite genius in too many realms to count. 'So, what are you going to do about it?'

'I told you, I'm going to do everything the right way this time. Just like humans do. I'll talk to her parents. Get them to give me her hand. In marriage.'

Mr B looked at him. Marriage?

'That's what people do.' Bob adopted his superior tone.

'How fascinating.' Mr B stared. 'Are you quite certain that's what you want?'

Bob snorted. 'Am I certain? Am *I* certain? Of course I'm certain. I'm beyond certain. I'm ridiculously certain.'

Mr B removed his spectacles and rubbed the bridge of his nose. 'Your mother is worried about you, you know.'

'My mother? *You've been talking to my mother?*'

'Only casually.'

Bob exploded. 'There is *no such thing* as a casual conversation with my mother. Every single word will be twisted beyond recognition until before you know it you're playing Russian Roulette in a wind tunnel with a psychotic dwarf, having wagered your birthright for a piece of cheese . . .'

Mr B blinked. 'Forget your mother. It was only a short chat.' He cleared his throat. 'There's a little favour I'd like to ask, however. A problem I need help solving.'

'No.' Bob pivoted on one superior heel and stormed out. The door slammed.

Mr B sighed. Bring on the fourteenth of July, he prayed, to no one in particular.

30

Bernard had always been a little shy about prayer. Having spent nearly twenty years as an army chaplain, he'd developed a definite unease about the job God was doing here on Earth. It was no surprise, therefore, that his bond with the Almighty, the most intense of his life, involved long and difficult conversations more than actual worship. And yet he wouldn't have chosen any other way to live, for he believed fervently in man's potential to improve life on Earth.

This was a political and philosophical belief as much as a spiritual one, requiring faith in concepts such as right and wrong, good and evil, salvation and grace. Bernard wanted very badly to believe that he and God had a single goal, and that the goal involved the eradication of suffering. Not that he believed, exactly, that suffering could be eradicated. But he believed in *the process*, the desire to make things better. Without human perfectibility as a goal, he could see no purpose to life on Earth.

In the early days of his career, he had considered the army good and useful and necessary. Even as that conviction waned, he had for many years felt that his presence in a war zone served a purpose, made life better for his men. When even that faded, he had returned to civilian life, and nowadays battled on the frontlines of the suburban middle class. His professional career, when he could bear to think about it, struck him as a slow tapering-off of worth.

Bernard had never been tempted to treat the Bible as literal truth, but all this vengeful weather disturbed him. Looking around the church at his parishioners, each valiantly trying to make the best of being marooned, he began to sag under a feeling of hopelessness. Perhaps the end of the world really was nigh.

'Hello, Mrs Edelweiss,' he said, pouring out a cup of tea. 'How are you this morning?'

She stared at him. 'How should I be, sleeping in a room full of strangers?'

Bernard flinched. 'Yes, of course, it's intolerable. But until we find you alternative housing, I'm afraid . . .' The woman was in her eighties, her hands twisted with arthritis. She should not be sleeping on a camp bed in a church hall, sharing four toilets with ninety others. 'We're doing our best to get you somewhere more comfortable, as soon as . . . look, the rain has –'

But as they both turned to the window, it was obvious that the rain hadn't. Only, it wasn't rain, as such. It looked as if the bottom of a lake had begun to spill over the church eaves. Bernard stared in wonder. The uninterrupted weight of water was dense as a wall.

Mrs Edelweiss was one of dozens around the room silently telegraphing the vulnerability and shame she felt at tolerating these conditions badly. Everywhere Bernard turned, he felt eyes upon him, apologetic, accusing. The old people had become accustomed to invisibility in a way the sturdy middle-aged were not; they had given over hope of being first in line for comfort or food or consolation. Their humility embarrassed Bernard. He checked his watch and grimaced, as if suddenly remembering an important engagement, then retreated to his tiny office behind the altar. He closed and locked the door and slumped into his chair. Un-Christian though the sentiment was, he wanted these people out of his church.

There came a tap on the door, and a familiar voice whispered, 'Bernard?'

He stood and unlocked it. 'Laura. Sorry. That wasn't meant to keep you out.'

A whiff of something distinctly Bernard puffed out at her as he opened the door – a hint of leather and candles and starched shorts; something arousingly vicarish. She handed him a cup of tea, wiping both hands on the apron she wore round her waist. 'Never mind. Tea and biscuits have been served, and we're all settling down to some nice Haydn quartets. Even the children are listening. Very good for the savage beast, you know.'

Breast, he thought, averting his eyes. Savage breast.

He pulled a chair out for her. 'Sit down for a moment. You've done too much.' Her efficiency implicated him somehow.

'I've actually come for a reason – more people have arrived and I thought you really ought to do the proper thing – welcome to Noah's ark, etc.'

'Yes, of course. Thank you.' He rose to his feet without enthusiasm. More refugees.

*

A youngish couple with two small children stood at the entrance to the church. The man, ginger-haired with freckles and pale eyes, put his hand out to Bernard.

'Hello, vicar. I'm afraid we've come for the high ground. Geographically speaking, that is.'

Bernard smiled. 'Please claim it however it serves you best.'

'We're stuck,' said his wife. 'Our kitchen's under half a metre of water, which,' she looked concerned, and even a little frightened, 'froze solid last night. In summer!' Indicating the two little girls, she added, 'This is Giselle, and Tamsin. I'm Rosalie. And Tom.'

'Welcome.' What a nice-looking family. Perhaps they'd come on Sundays when the emergency was over. They'd have to if they planned to get their little girls into St Anthony's C. of E. primary. Not for the first time, Bernard wondered who had less shame, the families playing this game, or the church insisting they play it.

Laura nudged him.

'There's someone else.'

He turned in the direction indicated by her chin.

'Hello,' he said. 'Can I help?'

'No.'

The vicar frowned. Something about this young man set the hairs on the back of his neck prickling, and his first impulse was to turn him straight back out into the rain. The muscles in his arms tensed. He opened his mouth to speak again, but was interrupted.

'Don't worry, I don't want your tea. I'm looking for her.' The young man pointed at Laura, his finger aimed at her nose.

Bernard's smile did not include his eyes. 'How fortunate, then, that you've found her.'

The young man ignored him, speaking directly to Laura. 'I need to talk to you.'

Mrs Davenport straightened her back, tipped her head slightly towards the ceiling and peered at the interloper along the short straight slope of her nose. In a pinch, she thought, I could probably take him. He may be young but he doesn't appear to be very fit. It wouldn't be difficult. Spike heel to instep, knee to groin, fingers in eyes (don't be afraid to gouge), heel of hand extended full force into Adam's apple. These thoughts distracted her, so that she barely noticed that the personage was speaking once more.

'I would like to discuss your daughter.'

She didn't recognize his accent. It appeared to contain a slight Russian inflection, or (could it be?) Chinese. And the slightest trace of – though perhaps she was mistaken – something Latin American? Portuguese?

'Which daughter?' Laura had no doubt which daughter he meant, though the thought of either of her children mixed up with such a creature made her shudder.

'Lucy.'

Lucy, of course. Carina's boyfriend was the son of an old family friend. Darling Carina, ambitious and unimaginative. A most restful sort of child. But Lucy . . . it figured that a girl with a compulsion for bringing home injured, abandoned and otherwise unsavoury mammals would somehow hook herself up with *this*. She stared at Bob with her hardest, coldest eyes. 'I'm Laura Davenport,' she said.

'I know who you are.' The young man glanced around. 'Is there somewhere we can talk?'

Could the boy actually have sneered a little? There was no mistaking the peculiar arrogance of his reply. Bernard had backed off to a tactful distance, watching the strange young man out of the corner of one eye. Now he took a step forward. 'Why don't you use my office? I'm happy to stay if you like, Laura.' His look was pointed.

'Thank you, but that shouldn't be necessary.' She drew back the corners of her mouth ever so slightly and spoke with an Arctic froideur. 'Follow me, . . .?'

'Bob.' He did not offer his hand.

'Bob.' She marched off towards Bernard's office, trusting the boy to follow. She left the door open. Neither sat.

She waited.

'I have an interest in your daughter.'

Of course he did. Lucy attracted a great deal of interest – what mother could possibly remain ignorant of that fact? Laura was somewhat disturbed by her daughter's wanton ability to arouse. So different from her own tidy sexuality.

'What sort of interest, precisely?'

'I am deeply and passionately in love with her.'

Deeply and passionately in love? The creature's use of language was as quaint as his accent – antique, almost, as if he'd studied with an Edwardian schoolmaster. She struggled to place him. Born in Hong Kong, perhaps? Educated at Eton? And why was it suddenly so hot? Long habits of discipline prevented her from clawing at her clothing, undoing every button and clasp. It will pass, she told herself. It will pass.

148

'And I believe I have made significant progress in winning her affections.'

'Why do you imagine your progress might interest me?' Laura's syntax acquired a patina of antiquity to match her opponent's. 'Lucy no longer lives at home and my influence over her, what little I have, does not include selecting her suitors. From what I understand, she is perfectly capable of organizing her social life entirely on her own, though of course I don't expect her taste to be suitable in every case.' She paused, giving him time to absorb the barb. 'In fact, I fail to comprehend the necessity for this conversation at all . . .'

Something extraordinary interrupted the flow of her lecture, and Laura could not be certain, then or later, exactly what that something was. Bob appeared to grow taller, and had it not been so patently unimaginable, she might have sworn that he began to morph, first into a dragon, then a gigantic cyclops, a minotaur, and a satyr of considerable height and breadth with eyes that glowed and hair shot through with fire. She blinked, wondering if perhaps she were having a stroke, squeezed her eyes shut and reopened them.

Bob stood before her exactly as he had a moment earlier. Well. She had obviously imagined it. Of course she had. And yet, why hadn't she noticed the peculiar intensity of him before? There was something at the core of him that felt as dense as the centre of the Earth. How had she failed to notice how he sucked all of the surrounding light into himself, swallowing it down until the edges of his figure glowed a fiery white?

Laura shook her head once more. Who *was* the boy? Even his eyes appeared to have changed colour and texture. Had they been molten amber before, threatening to flow out of his sockets like lava? She stared.

His voice was low, impatient. 'I should like to ask you for your daughter's hand,' he said, and when she looked alarmed, added, 'In marriage.' He stared at her expectantly and stood, cross-armed and impatient, tapping the floor with his foot.

As if from a trance, Laura came back to herself, feeling damp and slightly thick-headed. The room no longer felt unbearably hot. What if this peculiar boy-man were some sort of crazy stalker? She'd have to phone Lucy the moment he left.

Steadying herself against the wall, she took a deep breath. Lucy was a good girl. She always had been. Engaging and friendly. Her involvement with this strange person disturbed Laura greatly.

'The answer,' she said, 'is no. I'm afraid Lucy will have to make that sort of decision for herself . . . um . . . what did you say your name was?'

'Bob.'

'Bob . . . what?'

The young man didn't answer. He made no move to go.

'I should like to know . . .' she began. How had he found her? And what was all that odd – a cyclops? A minotaur? *Really?* She could barely form the questions that filled her brain. 'Did Lucy give you my address?' But this wasn't her address. She was in Bernard's church, more than a mile from home. 'I hope you don't mind if I ask whether my daughter is aware that you've come to see me today?'

'I don't mind at all,' said Bob, and disappeared.

31

Estelle observed her father patiently. 'Surely you can finish for the day,' she said. 'You've been working much too hard lately.'

'Too much to do, as ever,' Hed growled. He looked up at her. 'When did you get back?'

'Just now. And there is something I'd like to discuss with you.'

Hed grimaced. What had happened to the days when his daughter (or anyone else, for that matter) sought him out for the sole purpose of a pleasant chat? Nowadays it was all, 'Daddy, could you please' and 'Mr Hed, I have a proposition'. . .

He wondered what was coming next. Likely she wanted something. Oh blast, he thought. I hope she's not planning to go on about that idiot wager with Mona. Of course he had to go through with it now. And he supposed the sweetest meat in nine thousand galaxies was something to look forward to, even if it had to be swallowed along with his daughter's disapproval.

'Yes, Estelle?'

'I've been thinking, Daddy.'

'Admirable.' He scowled.

'I've been wondering about Bob. How he got his job.'

Hed's face registered surprise. Not what he'd been expecting at all. He rubbed his jaw. 'Well, I'd have to think. A poker game. Yes, definitely a poker game. Not one you attended. Mona won the job from me and passed it on to Bob.' If ever you needed proof of the evils of gambling, Hed thought. 'Why do you ask?'

'Just curious.'

The look Hed gave her was that of a man accustomed to discerning truth from untruth the way most men knew whiskey from gin. 'And?'

'And nothing.' Estelle's expression was mild.

He drummed his fingers on the desk impatiently.

'Well,' she said at last. 'What about me?'

'What *about* you?'

'Why didn't you offer the job to me?'

Hed sat up, genuinely astonished. 'It never crossed my mind.'

She waited.

'Of course, by all means, have a job if you like, but not that one. Nasty little place, gloomy location, miles from anywhere and completely buggered up by Mona's idiot son. Not the sort of thing suitable for you at all.' He stared at her some more. 'If you're wanting a position, I'll make enquiries, of course. But why not work for me? Handle my portfolio. Too many bits and pieces to manage properly these days, and impossible to get trustworthy stewards.' He sat back, eyes narrowed. 'Tell me, Estelle. You've said yourself how many interesting places and creatures you've encountered on your travels. So why this obsession with Earth?'

She thought for a moment. 'I've taken an interest in Earth because it needs help.'

'Demolition is what it needs,' growled Hed. 'Far too much of a mess to sort out now. And anyway, like it or not, that idiot Bob is God.'

'Forever?'

Hed shrugged. 'Who else would have him? Or it?'

Estelle hesitated. 'What if something were to change?'

Hed snorted. 'Exceptionally unlikely.'

Estelle was silent.

'Tell me,' her father said. 'What other things have you been thinking about?'

At this very moment, Estelle was thinking about her future. She had made up her mind long ago that the family business was not for her, for she was quite certain that she did not share her father's ruthless streak (though in this, she was substantially mistaken). Over a period of time, she had slowly been coming to a conclusion.

'I've been thinking about the Eck, Daddy.'

Hed closed his eyes, and his complexion darkened.

She waited, perfectly composed, till the shroud of smoke around him receded. 'I'm not asking you to do anything. You won him fair and square.'

'Fine. In which case, the conversation is closed. I never want to think about that idiot creature ever again. My chef is making arrangements for a nice pink peppercorn sauce to go with him. Though how he's supposed to know what sort of sauce is best for a creature he's never tasted . . .' Hed shrugged.

'But do you remember when I mentioned something in lieu?'

Hed's expression was stony.

'I didn't want you to think that I'd dropped the idea.'

'I hadn't thought about it. At all. To be perfectly frank.'

'Only . . .'

Hed glowered.

Estelle's smile, small and amused, nonetheless had the power to turn blood to ice. 'I am quite determined.'

'Determined, eh?' The look Hed aimed at his daughter contained more than a touch of menace. 'Determination can be a wonderful thing. And also utterly, totally pointless. If you get my drift.'

'Entirely, Daddy.'

'Well, then. Conversation over.'

Estelle stood and kissed him. 'I think you mean, "To be continued".'

Hed did not smile back. Except later. Just a little. To himself.

32

'You'll be glad to hear that my meeting with Lucy's mother went well.'

Eck looked up.

'I think she liked me.'

The little beast squinted, dubious.

'Though I don't suppose it matters, really. I'm God, she's not. I don't have to ask her anything. I'm just trying to do things the right way. Be polite. For Lucy's sake. Actually, to be perfectly honest, I don't give a damn if she approves or not.'

'Eck?' What about Lucy, he mused. I bet she cares.

Bob looked glum.

Though bursting with news about his new friend, Eck knew better than to share it. The effort of keeping the secret caused his nose to twitch.

Bob looked away, feigning indifference. 'You think Lucy's amazing, don't you?'

Eck shrugged. He hadn't seen enough of her to know. She clearly wasn't as amazing as *his* friend.

'And that we should be together forever?' Bob's eyes remained fixed on the window.

Eck hesitated. Forever seemed a strange concept to apply to a human. Lucy would live longer than he, a doomed Eck – but still, she was human. What would happen when she grew old and died?

And what about me, he wondered. Just a few weeks left. Will anyone miss me, or ever think of me when I'm dead? And does it matter? Will I even know?

He tried not to think about such things, but when he did, it was as if an imponderably large black hole had gaped open in his stomach and he was falling into it.

A shoe hit him in the temple and he yelped in pain.

'*Eck!*' He rubbed his head.

'That's what I thought too.' But Bob didn't appear cheered by this confirmation.

Whenever Eck thought about the world after he was gone from it, he felt dizzy and full of terror. An eternity dead, while the rest of the world went about its business not thinking about him at all – how could that be? It seemed cruel to him, being put on Earth just long enough to comprehend the full horror of extinction.

He'd tried to take the subject up with Bob. Why, he had asked, do I have to die?

In his heart of hearts, he'd been hoping that Bob would answer with an explanation of how he'd made an exception for his special pet; how, despite everything, Eck would live on into eternity – rather like the dodo in the Natural History Museum, he thought, only livelier.

But Bob hadn't corrected him. He hadn't laughed tolerantly and smacked him on the shoulder, and said, 'Don't be a dolt. Of course I'll make sure you live forever, you daft

Eck.' He hadn't even jabbed him in the ribs and reminded him about heaven or the afterlife. Bob had merely shrugged and turned back to the TV, and by the time he noticed Eck again it was obvious that he'd forgotten the question.

So the answer to the question about whether he would have to die, Eck gathered, was yes. Yes, he would have to die; yes, he would be forgotten and the world would go on forever without him. With no mitigating circumstances to make the horror easier to swallow.

It strained his relationship with Bob. Why did you bother creating me, he wanted to ask. Why bother giving me a brain and a realization of how miserable existence can be? Why did you invent creatures who die, and worse, who know they are going to die? What is the point of so unkind an act of creation?

But Bob hated difficult questions, and Eck's place in the household was tenuous enough already. For one thing, he ate too much. For another, he had an endless supply of questions. The funny thing was (only it didn't seem so funny to him) that being filled with questions only somehow made him feel emptier.

It didn't help that Bob had already placed an order for a new pet.

Mr B was somewhat kinder, making certain he had regular meals, and even giving him a pat once in a while. But no one seemed to take much of a serious interest. Dead Eck walking, that was him.

He tried to keep out of trouble, and occasionally thought about running away, finding another place to spend his last days. But his courage always failed him. He was just an Eck, and not a particularly fine specimen of an Eck, if what Bob told him was true. Without Bob, he wouldn't even have the dignity of being someone's pet.

'Nothing,' Bob said to him on any number of occasions. 'You are nothing.'

In his heart of hearts, Eck believed that he was nothing, for wouldn't God know about such matters?

Being nothing made him sad.

33

'Lucy, darling. You know I hate to pry, but, really, the man – the boy – was insupportably rude.' Worse than rude. 'I'm not entirely sure how to describe it –'

At the other end of the telephone, Lucy made an impatient sound. 'Is there anything else? Because I don't want to talk about it.'

'Well, no . . . there's nothing else, and I can understand perfectly that you don't want to talk about it. I don't want to talk about it either, in point of fact. Only, he did come looking for me, hunting me down, if you must know. And he asked me for your hand in marriage . . . which you have to admit is a trifle odd.'

Marriage? Lucy trembled. Marriage? *Oh my God.*

'Lucy?'

'Yes, I'm here.'

'In this day and age, darling? Why approach me? He barely knows you, and he certainly doesn't know me. And how did he know where to find me? You say you didn't give him the address and, even if you had, he didn't find me at home. I don't like it, darling. It feels wrong.'

'He asked permission to marry me. Some parents might consider that a nice thing.'

Laura sighed. 'It's not *what* he asked, darling, it's how.'

'Are you suggesting that wanting to marry me makes him some sort of sociopath, Mother? A pervert? *Do you want me to call the police*, Mother?'

'Of course not.' Though Laura wondered if perhaps that wouldn't be such a bad idea. 'I'm only thinking of you.'

'Look, Mother, if it makes you feel better, I'll investigate, find out all about him. One of my friends knows his family,' she lied.

'Which friend?'

'Oh for heaven's sake,' Lucy said, thinking of the skinny, rather unprepossessing boy of her dreams. 'Are you suggesting that he's dangerous?'

Laura frowned. Odd, unpleasant, inappropriate, surreal? Yes. But dangerous?

Yes.

She could see him clearly now – the childish manner, the weird density of him, with something threatening underneath, something violent and peevish.

'Goodbye, Mother.' Lucy put down the phone. It was so typical of her mother to be suspicious of anyone who wasn't part of her circle, anyone different from the ambitious, ordinary sons of her friends. He loves me. Why couldn't she understand that?

And yet . . . Lucy could not pretend to be free of doubt. She tried to push it out of her head. Was she the sort of girl who got what she wanted only to run away? He'd said he loved her. He'd said it.

But who *was* he?

Bob considered the encounter with Lucy's mother. Their exchange of ideas had been a good start, he thought, though he'd much rather have reduced her to a thimbleful of ash.

He trembled at the thought of Lucy; a bubble of happiness exploded in his chest. *We*, he thought. Lucy and me: *together*. He marvelled at the power of this human girl to make the terrible solitude of his life recede. This was what happiness felt like – this wondrous, miraculous alternative to dread.

He needed to set the scene, to keep her love safe in a bottle, like a firefly.

All of this thinking frustrated him. So much to organize. If only Mr B were a proper sort of helper, *he* could do it, take a few moments out of his frantic schedule of sick children or raped women or whatever his boo-hoo cause of the week happened to be.

Bob rolled his eyes. Sick, starving, it was all the same. He couldn't see what the big deal was. Any observer with half a brain knew that there'd always been an underclass – serfs, slaves, untouchables – and, furthermore, that they probably deserved their horrible fates. He hated that Mr B wasted all his time (valuable time the man could be spending on, like, *hello*, me?) fussing over the huddled masses like some pathetic old hermit granny do-gooder.

He knocked at Lucy's window. She came slowly and peered out into the grey incessant rain and the tide of water below her, uncertain, expecting no one. When she saw it was Bob, she smiled, but her greeting was guarded.

'I've just stopped by . . . I just hoped . . . would you like to have a picnic with me?'

Despite herself, Lucy giggled. 'In this weather? Shall I wear a wetsuit?'

The thought of Lucy in a wetsuit struck him speechless for a moment. 'Um. That won't be necessary. We'll have sunshine by Saturday.'

She laughed then. 'Oh, really? What are you? Some kind of weatherman?'

'Some kind,' he mumbled.

Her face became solemn once more. 'So, a picnic. On a boat?'

'Yes,' he said firmly. 'On a boat.'

Lucy paused, considered her reservations, then pushed them aside. 'OK, Mr Weatherman. A picnic on a boat it is. Shall I bring the picnic?'

'Yes, perfect! I'll bring the boat.' Could she hear his exultation in the silence that followed? 'OK. Well. See you Saturday, then.'

Neither of them moved.

'Look, Bob . . .'

'Lucy . . .'

They both stopped. The rain paused, droplets hovering uneasily in mid-air.

'Lucy,' he began, taking both her hands. 'Lucy, I know we haven't known each other long, but . . .'

'Bob, I'm not sure . . .'

'But I feel terrible when I'm not with you.' He released her and ran one distraught hand through his hair. 'I'd leave you alone if I could, but I can't . . . I can't *breathe* without you. I don't think you understand how unhappy I've been.'

When their eyes met, the charge nearly knocked her over. What *was it* about him? She didn't even seem to have a choice; he needed her and so she needed him back. It was terrifying and exhilarating at once, like riding the crest of a gigantic wave.

They stood together but apart, both trembling, and then slowly she stepped forward and laid her head against his shoulder. He tightened his arms round her and the grey afternoon peeled away, exposing a soft pink summer sky of extraordinary beauty, radiant with warm amber light. Bob was Midas, turning the world to gold; in his arms, Lucy glowed. As the moments passed, the space around them melted and blurred, and it became impossible to tell where one of them ended and the other began.

'I'll think of something,' Bob murmured, kissing her hair. 'I'll think of a way we can be together. I will.'

And then he pulled back from her and smiled, and his smile sealed her in a lozenge of bright warmth.

A little dazed, Lucy moved away. The pale oval of her face lingered, flickering for a few seconds after she closed the shutters and disappeared. Bob reached his hand out to grasp her, but touched only air.

He stood motionless at the window for a long moment. It was late of course, but he was far too wound up to go home. Every particle of him fizzed with desire, with something greater than desire.

He thought of Mr B and the usual dinner with the usual conversation. 'You haven't', 'you didn't', 'you should have'.

According to Mr B, he embodied all the deadly sins: indolence, lust, a refusal to clear up his room, crankiness (well, who wouldn't be?), insubordination, dyslexia . . . how many was that? Normally he didn't much care what Mr B thought of him, but today, this minute, bathed in the silvery shimmer of Lucy light, he couldn't bear the thought of returning to his ordinary life.

He found a boat and pushed off into the soft still radiant dusk.

34

Mr B hadn't seen Bob in hours and, pleasant as the experience was, he had begun to feel nervous.

Where could the boy be? Mr B didn't like Out There, especially after dark. The complications of nightclub bouncers, marauding wolves and armed gangsters unsettled him; dark alleys and swooping bats sent him scurrying back home to a nice supper of steak and peas and all that was familiar and brightly lit. It wasn't that he was frightened of the dark, exactly. He was frightened of how Bob's creatures ran amok in the dark. Gangs and guns and attack dogs were the consequence of his creations' aggressive paranoia, yet another flaw that Bob hadn't quite anticipated in his design of *Homo sapiens*.

What would happen if Bob failed to return? Measures would have to be taken. He rubbed his forehead. But which measures? You couldn't just take to the streets with a sandwich board proclaiming that you'd misplaced the Heavenly Father. A search was in order, but how, and where to start?

Lucy, obviously. Damn the girl. And damn the vast frothing juggernaut of Bob's sex drive. For a very few moments, Mr B had dared to hope that this particular romantic adventure might not end in cataclysm. But what would change the pattern of a history as long as theirs?

With a huge sigh, he pulled on a dusty waxed canvas raincoat, tugged on a pair of wellies and flipped the Victorian-style collar up over his ears. Lord only knew what sort of weather he'd encounter. The stiff coat creaked round him like a tent, its folds rendering him smaller and less significant, even, than usual.

From his window he could see that a sailboat had dropped anchor in their road. He slowly unfurled his black umbrella. Two of its ribs pointed crazily sideways.

Despite the extreme unlikelihood of finding Bob swinging along the tops of the lampposts like Gene Kelly (a song in his heart and ready for love), Mr B still peered up the canal that had once been a street.

There was nothing.

Mr B hated so many of man's wondrous creations: engines and mobile phones and fast-food outlets, not to mention knives and jackhammers and garrottes. In the past, he had hated crossbows and armour and coins. Pisspots. And instruments of torture. He loathed the noise and smell of Outside – the roaring vehicles with their damp diesel stink, which clung to his skin, and the horrible whine of planes slicing up the sky. To him these things represented everything sordid and backwards about Earth.

'No, Eck.' He pushed the little creature's snout out of the crack of the door and closed it behind him.

A dinghy awaited him and he stepped into it.

The peculiar dazzle of city nightlight caused him to blink. He shuddered as his boat slid past an old woman balanced on a windowsill, gazing blank-faced at the rising water. They were so close that he could smell the rotting human scent of her through the plastic sweet camellia of her perfume. She smiled at him and he turned away, ashamed.

At Lucy's there was no sign of Bob, thank goodness. Just a nice girl tucked up in bed asleep. After the first wave of relief, Mr B felt stirrings of panic. Where next? Where could he be? Bob's incurious nature meant that he rarely wandered aimlessly. Would he bother cruising for women, replace Lucy before the object had been achieved? Mr B knew him better than that. His passion might fade in a matter of hours or days – but not now, not yet.

He headed for high ground, searching bars and pool halls, red-light districts and clubs. He asked phony wise men on the tops of real mountains whether anyone had come through seeking advice for the lovelorn. He checked strip clubs and casinos on six continents. He peered into the dark corners of opium dens and coffee shops, interviewed any number of all-night bartenders and working girls, wandered along the observation platforms of the Empire State Building and the World Financial Center in Shanghai, took the lift to the top of the Burj Khalifa. And, finally, he gave up, exhausted by failure, frustrated by the difficulties thrown up by seven billion identikit creatures of Bob's design.

No sleep was possible. He didn't feel like going home.

As he paddled steadily through the outskirts of the city, the artificial light slipped away and, with it, the trapped-fly buzz of humanity. He stopped for a moment, drifting in silence through the drizzle. The moon had just begun to rise, a great orange disc, majestic and strange. Little boats manned by dark silhouettes bobbed in the floodwater; soft voices came to him across the land that was no longer land. Mr B sat motionless, mesmerized by the tiny percussion of raindrops, plinketytink, like plucked strings. A path of silver moonbeam crossed the floodwater towards him and he slipped into it, shifting his paddle so that he drifted along its length. He felt he might follow it forever.

How beautiful it is, he thought. The entire world appeared to have paused on an in-breath.

His and Bob's rather spartan flat offered little opportunity to appreciate nature, except perhaps in memoriam – the beauty of what had once been, recorded now in prayers aimed at them from every corner of the world. Save the tigers, save the oceans, save the ice-caps. The images he saw all arose out of catastrophe.

But just for a moment he viewed the place in terms of what could be. And on this night, it was impossible not to notice that the world was touched with magic. In this moment he felt a suspension of despair, a ceasefire in the world's torment. Stars burned silver in the great black sky, carrying messages to Earth from a billion miles away. No horizon split the seamless night. Not a person would petition him to change this moment. It just was, and it was good. And for a moment he too was good.

On the other side of the flood lake, Bob hung facedown over the edge of his little rowing boat, nose nearly touching the water, fingers leaving silver trails in the dark. It was nice out here. The night seemed created just for him, full to bursting with the possibility that something wonderful might happen quite soon: sex, fulfilment and love, all wrapped up in one beautiful sparkly package. After he had opened the package he would be happy ad infinitum, and nothing would ever disturb him again so long as he had Lucy and her love.

For they *would* be together, that much he knew for certain. All that was left to figure out were the details of their shared life. He wasn't accustomed to organizing things without Mr B, but it couldn't be that difficult; if the old codger could do it, he could. He would find a place for them to live happily ever after.

No world was as beautiful as this world he'd created, Bob thought, none so delicately poised between life and death. Mr B might berate the short-lived race he'd made, berated it all the time, in fact. But he was proud of the experiment, proud of the weird evanescence all those short lives produced. OK, maybe it wasn't so nice for them, but at least they didn't drag along day after bloody day, always the same. Always alone.

Would it really be better, he wanted to ask, if it were always this nice? Would anyone bother to notice? Or would they simply pass through a night like this, unmoved?

And (this was more to the point) if life were without flaws and no one ever changed or died, what role would God have?

A muffled sound of voices reached him. Above, the stars glittered so large and bright, he thought he might throw a net and pull them towards him like whiting. Boats slid past him in the inky dark but failed to enter his thoughts.

Mona stared at the oily water through the shell of a bobbing glass egg. The moonlight depressed her. She didn't like her son's sordid little planet, felt guilty for him and Mr B, so wrong was the pairing.

It was all the fault of the damned gambling.

Many years ago, a bet had led her to marry off one of her daughters to a vast shapeless draw-hole of infinite gravity who had (understandably, Mona thought at the time) been finding it difficult to establish a permanent relationship. Mona never saw that particular daughter again, but even without the girl's reproach she knew she'd done wrong.

It was another bet that landed a rather sweet ex-boyfriend in eternal slavery at the far reaches of Cygnus A. Another game resulted in a particularly unpleasant weekend for Mona in the company of the most obnoxious creature in the Pinwheel Galaxy – a gigantic slimy beast with thousands of groping fronds.

Mona's little glass egg wobbled a little on the wake of a passing boat. She looked up at the handsome young man at the helm, realizing with a start that it was her son. She sat up. When he wasn't sneering and whining, he looked . . . quite beautiful. The unformed quality of his features would improve with age. But would he ever grow up?

Mr B spotted Mona's illuminated egg and managed to catch her eye. She waved as they drifted past one another, Mona receding in the night until she was nothing but a lazy glow.

Seeing Mona brought Mr B's thoughts back to Bob, his insistent denial of the future. How could he fall in love with one of his creations and expect it to end happily? Who knew better than he what happened to them over time? Who, after all, had created the poor things, making no provision for the retention of beauty and hope? Not to mention hair, eyesight, hearing, the ability to walk, control of the sphincter.

A sliver of guilt pricked Mr B. What if Bob had got wind of his resignation? What if he'd found out and felt betrayed by what was, after all, a colossal betrayal?

In the distance he caught a final glimpse of Mona's glowing egg and suddenly his heart felt heavy and inert. Had he ever been happy? Would he ever be happy again?

How can I leave this world to Bob? Who will guide him in the care and feeding of his unhappy planet? Who will instruct him in what little could be done to improve life for its inhabitants? Who will tolerate his extremes of stupidity, stick by him through thick and thin (mainly thick)? Who will instruct him in the subtleties of responsibility, kindness, self-control? Mr B sighed, removed his spectacles, wiped his eyes.

Estelle drifts by in her little boat, near enough for Mr B to see that she cradles something in her lap. It is the Eck, a softly purring Eck, eyes twitching and half-closed with bliss as she strokes him. She murmurs sweet words to him and he wriggles a little, snuggling closer; the sound he makes isn't one Mr B has ever heard before – a sigh of such perfect complexity that it rewrites everything he has imagined Bob's pet capable of feeling.

Something about this scene ignites a tiny flame in Mr B's heart and he cannot tear his eyes from it. Estelle is not beautiful – but the pure clarity of her features makes her as irresistible to him as an angel. He would like to be in the boat with them, in the place of the Eck. He would like to be held in the arms of this clear-eyed, clear-voiced girl, who seems to be the only creature among all his acquaintances who cares for something besides self-glorification and the gratification of her own desires.

It might cause considerable surprise to the informed observer (who does not exist) to note that Mr B's eyes begin to fill with tears. They overflow and spill down along the deep soft creases of his careworn face as he sits very still in the centre of the unstill world and weeps rivers of salty water for all the lost souls, including his own.

Seven comets streak across the dawn.

35

By the time Saturday arrived, the sun was blazing and Mr B felt marginally more hopeful.

Bob finally emerged from his room, dressed in jeans and trainers, sunglasses, an expensive T-shirt and a cashmere sweater. He'd slung a jacket and straw bag over one shoulder in an attempt to look French and posed for a moment by the window, his right profile artistically in shade. After a few seconds, he spun round, enquiringly.

Mr B didn't look up. '*Très jolie.*'

Bob slammed the door on his way out.

The weather was holding up nicely, Bob thought, arranging a great bed of Moroccan cushions in the sunshine. He gave his felucca a little push off the side of the building and floated off, testing it for comfort, throwing himself down upon the bed of pillows, clasping his hands beneath his head and closing his eyes against the sun. Wow, he thought. This would be nice even without Lucy.

Creation looked pretty damned impressive in good weather. Big sun, blue sky, fluffy white clouds; the trees artistic shades of orange, red and gold. Even the flood sparkled and winked with diamonds of reflected light. Birds chirped. Bob frowned. His world was perfectly fine. Gorgeous, in fact. And he never got any credit for it. It was so typical. Nothing he did was ever good enough. It was *so unfair*.

He glanced at his watch. Almost noon. Time to pick up his girlfriend. *His. Girlfriend.* Were there two more beautiful words in any language? With the sweep of a giant oar, he turned the boat towards Lucy's house. It slipped silently through town, past a vast flotilla of less noteworthy craft, until at last it bumped gently against the corner of Lucy's first-floor flat. He could see his true love through the window, everything about her redolent of freshness and beauty and life.

When she saw Bob's boat, Lucy clapped a hand to her mouth in delight. Bob bowed and she opened the French doors, stepping out on to her balcony and then on to the edge of the felucca. He offered a hand to help her and for a moment they clung tightly to each other as the boat rocked. Steadying himself, Bob shoved the boat off the corner of the building and they were adrift.

'It's magic,' Lucy murmured. 'Where on earth did you get it?'

'Egypt,' Bob answered, concentrating hard on steering them into open water. 'From the Nile.'

Lucy frowned. 'No, seriously,' she said.

'Seriously.' He met her eyes with a steady gaze. She smiled, a little doubtfully.

'Sit down, sit down,' he commanded gaily. 'You'll tip us if you kneel on one side like that.'

She sat.

The weather was perfect. People on every street hung out of windows, grinning, calling to one another, delighted by the return of sunshine and the unexpected warmth. Even in a world of boats, Bob's barge did not escape notice. There were catcalls and wolf-whistles from the men. Children and young women waved, hoping for a ride. Lucy, glowing, unpacked sandwiches and a bottle of wine while Bob guided the craft round a corner, its oar set slightly to one side.

What a wonderful adventure, she thought. Imagine, showing up at my window with such a beautiful boat!

On the other hand, it was strange. No one she knew had money for a boat like this. Did he come from a rich family? Was he a drug dealer? A bank robber? Was he one of those Eurotrash types you read about in *Hello!* with a year-round tan and a huge bank balance? Did it matter?

When Bob's hand slid under her hip to arrange the rug for her, she allowed his fingers to press against her as she swept her soft lashes towards the sky.

They drank and they ate and they kissed. After all the rain, they lolled tipsy in the sunshine, which warmed their faces and filled their limbs with the sense of something rare and uncanny.

I am God, thought Bob. The almighty all-powerful God. And what a smashing good world I've created, complete with this gorgeous girl. What a *brilliant* realm of pleasure. What a beautiful flood. What perfect sunshine. What a fabulous genius of a boyfriend I am.

He lowered himself down beside Lucy, pushed his arm under her head and rubbed his cheek against hers. The two giggled and joked and touched, skin to skin, giddy with happiness, igniting currents of pleasure on every exposed surface. After weeks spent dodging the wind and rain, warm sun against warm flesh upon warm wool felt like a benediction.

Bob and Lucy gazed at each other, and each thought silently that this was the moment to which all other moments had led. Bob looked at Lucy and knew – he *knew* – that with her by his side he would never be lonely again, would never again suffer the heart-wrenching isolation of his position. Lucy would share every aspect of his life, the good and the bad; she would love him and be loved. Yes, she was mortal, but perhaps – *why not?* – perhaps he would renounce the position of God for her! It wasn't exactly fun any more. To tell the truth, each year seemed drearier than the one before. Who could have guessed that his wondrous creation would generate so many problems? Enough, he thought. Enough responsibility, enough nagging! Why had he never before thought of quitting the whole enterprise? As the idea came to him, it filled him with hope.

Perhaps it was the wine, perhaps it was love's sweet intoxication, but the plan Bob unspooled for Lucy swept them both along on a wave of optimism. A picture formed in their heads as they drifted along aimlessly in the sunshine, and it was the same picture for both – of freedom and happiness forever.

'Lucy, dear Lucy.' Bob's voice cracked, as if it were a huge effort to speak at all. 'You are the world's most wondrous woman.'

'I'm not,' she whispered back. 'You've just lost your mind, that's all.'

He nodded. 'I have.'

His eyes made her dizzy, but her expression, now, was serious. 'You might tire of me in a week, a month.' She put her hand on his arm, turned her mouth to his.

'Never,' he murmured, believing with every fibre of his glorious being that their love was indeed eternal, that he and Lucy would be together forever and ever and ever – forever, that is, until she grew old and infirm, lame and deaf and crotchety, until bits began falling off her and she withered up and started to smell funny and developed arthritis and arteriosclerosis. And then died. Which would be relatively soon, when you compared her lifespan to his.

She turned, half sat and looked at him, really looked, determined to find out what lay behind his strangeness. His eyes were like quicksand, pulling her down and under, where she had nothing to grasp. And yet a tiny scrap of her refused to succumb entirely; a tiny scrap of instinct whispered: danger.

'I feel . . .' She hesitated. 'When I'm with you, I can't imagine being anywhere else. And yet . . .' She glanced away, and then back, baffled.

He smiled.

Lucy shook her head. 'I don't know how to understand it.' She was earnest. It all made sense to her now, the empires lost for love, the families and fortunes sacrificed. If this is love, she thought, I have grossly underestimated the power of it.

Bob watched her, and knew that he too had been wrong

about the world. It had been veiled even from him, its creator, and now lay before him in a fullness of glory.

Did I create this too? And if I'd done it better or different, would Lucy exist?

He drew her hand gently to his cheek and pressed it there, kissing her wrist. If they could merge into a single entity, then everything would be peaceful for all time. For what seemed like hours they kissed sweetly, indolently.

Gradually he became more urgent. 'Marry me, Lucy. Sleep with me,' he whispered, nuzzling her ear, her hair, her neck.

She pressed against him, wanting nothing more than his body against hers.

He looked at her. 'Let's elope.'

She almost laughed, but stopped when she saw that he meant it. How could she not be tempted by these prospects, torn between elation and a niggling voice of fear? How could she not?

'You went to see my mother,' she said.

For an instant he looked stricken. 'I want everyone to know how we feel. How serious I am. The whole world. Not just you.'

The afternoon was fading. Lucy said nothing as he guided the boat towards her home. At the door, Bob lingered, taking hold of her shoulders. 'You haven't answered me,' he said, his voice soft.

She shook her head.

'Promise me you'll think about it,' he whispered, and she nodded. 'I'll let you go, now.' He did not release her, but kissed her, again.

'Yes,' she said, her lips against his mouth. And then again, at last, with perfect certainty, 'Yes.'

'Yes?' He tries to say more, but joy renders him speechless. And what happens between them is not like any description of any act of love that she has ever read or heard about or seen. She imagines that this is what it is to be infinite, flying and lost, with no past or future. The pleasure she feels is at once infinitely reassuring and infinitely dangerous, and when it is finished she wants it to start all over again, or never to end.

'I love you, Lucy,' he says, kissing her eyes. 'Let's run away.'

What she experiences with Bob short-circuits her brain. She feels as fragile as the filament of a bulb, as flickering and evanescent. 'Run away where?' Was he madly in love, or just mad? Was love meant to be so much like falling?

He hesitates, casting about wildly. 'A place I know. A little place far from anywhere and anyone else.' He thinks of a planet he once visited, ten billion light years away. 'It belongs to a friend.' He catches her look of doubt. 'He hasn't used it in years. It would be as good as ours.'

'I'll think about it.' And she speaks the truth, for she will be able to think of nothing else – a little place, and just the two of them. Perhaps, a cosy stone cottage, a warm fire, a view of the sea . . . with this astonishing feeling and the beautiful boy who loves her to distraction.

And the slim blade of anxiety that hovers, inexorably, over the scene.

For now, she wants him to go. So she can think about everything that has happened.

He kisses her goodbye with such tenderness that her limbs

can barely support her weight. When finally he is gone, she melts down the wall and sits, hugging her knees, a little dazed with the knowledge of exactly how much sex simplifies and complicates everything.

36

Bob's success in mortal-style seduction left him feeling triumphant – he paddled slowly through the night in his beautiful boat, light and powerful, keen as a laser.

'Hello, my darling.'

He shrieked and leapt over the side of the boat with a great splash.

'So sorry, my sweet, did I startle you?'

Climbing back aboard, he spluttered, 'Yes. Now please go.'

Mona put on her most engaging pout. 'But I've only just arrived. And, look, you've got just enough wine left for a teensy little –'

Dripping and furious, he snatched the bottle from her hand.

'Never mind the drink, then.' Mona's smile looked strained. 'Well, so! She certainly seems like a lovely girl. The hair, the smile, the whole . . .' She indicated helplessly. 'But if you'll just . . .'

Bob turned away. 'Just what? Oh, I get it – you noticed that I'm a teensy bit less suicidal than usual and you've come to fix that?'

Mona sighed. 'The thing is, my darling – she's mortal.

Not her fault, obviously, but a problem nonetheless. Think about it. Thirty years from now, when she's fifty-one and you're . . . you're the same as ever.'

'So what?'

'OK, not thirty years. Forty years. Sixty. She'll be a decrepit old mortal and you'll be exactly the same as you are now. Nineteen? Twenty? I'm so terrible with birthdays.' Mona peered at him, offering a small sympathetic smile. 'It never works, my darling.'

'I'll make it work.'

'Oh, but, my sweet, you won't.' She dipped her head in sympathy. 'How many mortals have you been with? One? Ten?'

He glared. 'How many have *you* been with?'

Mona smiled and averted her gaze. 'Oh, heaven knows. I've lost count. I do like mortals, that's true.' When she turned back to him, her expression was serious. 'But I'd never fall in love with one. Imagine the explaining you'd have to do. Think of the look on Lucy's face when you tell her who you are.'

Bob's bravado dropped suddenly and his eyes filled with tears. His shoulders sagged. 'You don't want me to be happy.'

His mother's face was all tenderness. She placed an arm round him, drawing him close. 'Of course I do, my darling. Of course I want you to be happy. But not like this. This won't make you happy. And it won't make her happy either. In actual fact, it will probably scare her to death.'

Bob wanted to spend forever with Lucy – he did not want their relationship to end with the sort of mistakes he had made in the past. He would not appear in her bedroom as a vast pawing bull, or a ten-foot eagle with scales. He did not want Mr B to dispose of her afterwards, when he tired of the game. So, he was immortal and she wasn't . . . their relationship could still work. He'd make it work.

For a moment he imagined himself her equal, with nothing between them but true love and a long peaceful future. Surely, as God, he could manage that?

Mona watched him, the conflict on his face writ large. 'Sweetheart?'

Bob swung round and glared at her. 'Go away.'

'I know some very nice goddesses –'

'No.'

'Only, they're really quite nice. And immortal.'

'Great. So if I don't like them I'm stuck with them hanging around forever.'

Mona sighed deeply and Bob veered on to the offensive. 'Do you think you have even the faintest *clue* about the sort of girl I'm attracted to? Don't make me laugh.' He laughed, bitterly.

The thought of a girl chosen for him by his mother was, frankly, repulsive. He could see her exactly. She'd either be hideously prim or a good-time girl like his mother (which would be far, far worse). She'd be possessed of a too-eager smile, big white teeth and a thick cardigan. Or twelve heads and big leathery paws. Either way he felt sick. Whatever girl his mother might dig up for him was definitely not a girl he wanted to meet, much less spend the rest of his life with.

'Darling,' she began, and something in her tone made him pause. 'I want you to be happy. I want it more than anything. And if I could pull some strings, or beg some higher power to allow you and Lucy to live happily ever after, I would.

But it doesn't work like that, my darling.'

Bob stared at her. 'But I love her.'

'I know you do. I'm sorry.' She embraced him and stroked his hair. 'I'm so sorry,' she murmured.

Bob broke away. He swept one hand roughly over his eyes, brushing away the tears. His expression hardened. 'I'll make it work,' he said. 'Mr B will help me.'

Mona hesitated. 'Did it ever occur to you that your Mr B might not always be around to help you?'

He looked at her as if she were mad. 'No, of course it never occurred to me. Of course he'll always be here. It's his job.'

She wanted to tell him that it was time to take control of his own life and his own planet because quite soon there would be no one else to do it for him. But she lacked the appetite for confrontation and, in any case, what the hell. It would all turn out fine no matter what. Lucy or no Lucy . . . who would even remember in a hundred years?

'Perhaps you're right after all, darling. You and Lucy, together forever.' Mona threw her hands up as if tossing caution, quite literally, to the wind. 'Live the dream! Go for it!' And she laughed her best devil-may-care laugh.

But Bob had lost interest – he was gazing, fascinated, at the brightly graffitied wall of an old brick warehouse as the felucca drifted slowly past. On it was written:

THERE IS NO GOD

37

A safari park on the outskirts of town had been calling all week looking for places for a couple of young lions, twenty-two gazelle and an entire herd of zebras.

Luke rolled his eyes. 'What'd you tell them?'

'I told the guy to stuff them in a taxi and send them over.' Mica made a gun with one hand and pointed it at his right temple.

'OK, thanks. Any other crises?'

'Other than the obvious, no, but you'd better give him a ring. I turned him down in every language I could think of and he didn't seem to be taking it in.'

Luke nodded and took the Post-it note with the number scrawled on it. He felt sorry for the safari park, but another week of meteorological freakery and he'd be in exactly the same position.

'What're you doing here so early, anyway?' He glanced at his watch. It wasn't much past 6 a.m., only just light outside and drizzling.

'You said you'd sack me if I didn't start keeping the same hours as you.'

Luke nodded absently. He'd been working sixteen-hour

days for God knew how long, trying to make up for the shortage of staff and the excess of problems. 'Thanks for coming in. I appreciate it.'

'You bloody well should. I hate mornings. Getting in at nine was bad enough.'

'You'll go to heaven, Mica.'

Mica put a hand on Luke's arm and batted his eyes. 'Only if you take me.'

But Luke wasn't listening. He'd come into work on Saturday in a state of elation. Sun, everywhere. It was straight out of some demented cola advert. Not boiling hot, not freezing cold, no hail or sleet or snow. Just a perfect beautiful breezy sunny day. Even the reptiles in their dim homes must have felt something in the change of barometric pressure – snakes and lizards he hadn't seen for days, weeks, had emerged to sit on branches and blink.

This is too good to last, he'd thought. And it hadn't.

Now he saw Lucy on the other side of the courtyard, hauling a flat trolley loaded with four bales of straw through the greyish drizzle. Something about her (was it the hunch of her shoulders?) appeared less buoyant than usual. Perhaps it was going badly with the strange boyfriend. Without an ounce of guilt, Luke hoped so. Not that he was interested in her, but he wouldn't have liked any of his staff hanging around with that guy.

What was it about women, he wondered, that they fancied such obvious losers? What could Lucy possibly see in Bob, besides the good looks of a serial womanizer? The vibes he gave off chilled Luke's blood, and he didn't like the thought of them together. OK, so Lucy had never been his favourite employee, but it was impossible to miss the fact that she'd been utterly steadfast throughout the crisis, not once claiming an inability to get to work. Perhaps he'd underestimated her.

He trotted through the gloom and took the handle of her trolley. She forced a smile. 'I'm fine,' she said, attempting to take the load back from him. 'It's not that heavy.'

But he held fast and they walked in silence through the rain. 'I'd have killed to get anyone in at this hour a few weeks ago,' he said at last. 'Maybe the weather's not such a bad thing after all.'

'Oh,' she sighed. 'Don't even joke about it. I felt so happy on Saturday when I thought it might actually be over.' When I had sex with Bob. Amazing sex. Or was it love? Amazing love? Either way, he hadn't called. Why hadn't he called? Even without a phone, he should have goddamned called. He said he'd find me.

Together they heaved and shoved the bales into the storage bin.

'Thanks.' Lucy looked uncomfortable. 'But I'm perfectly fine doing it myself.'

'Mmm.' Luke stood for a minute, considering the checklist in his head. Food deliveries had been sporadic this week; they'd have to start thinking about emergency rations. The pigs seemed listless and the heating in the camel's enclosure was on the blink. He'd managed to borrow a horse rug to keep the animal warm, but hadn't counted on the difficulties of getting the camel to stand still while they fastened it. The usually placid beast kicked and shrieked whenever they approached, shivering with cold and fear till Luke was ready to wring his s-bend neck.

He looked up and found Lucy staring at him with a slightly puzzled expression. 'Don't look so worried,' he said. 'I'm just having a quiet panic about getting through the week.'

She shrugged. 'We'll help.'

'Yes.' He turned to go, but on second thoughts turned back. 'Thanks,' he said, as if he meant it this time. 'I know you will.'

38

'Darling . . .'

Bob groaned.

Mr B looked up from his work. 'Hello, Mona. You're looking charming, as ever.' She was dressed in what appeared to be a few strands of seaweed.

'Do you like it? Straight off the catwalk.' She spun round.

Bob mimed two fingers down his throat accompanied by hairball gagging, and turned away.

'Gorgeous, Mona.'

'Excuse me.' Bob's face wore an expression of outraged incredulity. 'When you two fossils have finished exchanging pleasantries, do you think you might pay attention to me and my plight?'

Mona turned to him, her face a picture of maternal sympathy. 'I'm so sorry, sweetheart,' she said. 'Remind me again what your plight is?'

Bob rolled his eyes. 'Hello? *Lucy?* My one and only transcendent true love? Am I so *completely insignificant* that you *can't even recall* our last conversation?'

'It's not that at all, not one bit, dear one. It's just that I thought we'd resolved that particular question . . .'

'The question of my heart? Of the only possibility for happiness I'll ever have?'

Mona coughed a little. 'Darling boy. You know I worry about your happiness. Which is why I'm afraid I'm going to have to forbid you to see Lucy ever again.'

Bob stared at her, aghast.

'Yes, forbid you. No more mortals.' She reached over and patted his arm, shooting a furtive glance at Mr B, who looked away. 'Mother knows best.'

'Don't be absurd,' he choked. 'You can't stop me.'

'Well, I can, obviously.' Mona smiled modestly.

Bob's eyes swivelled wildly. 'You would actually *sabotage* my relationship?'

'Sabotage?' Mona appealed to Mr B. 'Have you ever known me to indulge in sabotage?'

The older man shrugged. He had certainly known her to indulge in chaos and pandemonium. Not to mention carelessness and drunk and disorderly conduct. But sabotage? Not that he could remember offhand. 'Though a bit of sabotage,' he mused aloud, 'might be just the ticket at the mo–'

The noise that emerged from Bob's mouth shattered every window in the room.

Bob tore at his hair and rent the hem of his garment. He was God, the Almighty, the All-powerful Everlasting Father, King of Kings and Lord of Lords. With the Mother of all Mothers.

Mona waved and disappeared, throwing a kiss that appeared to encompass them both while Bob stormed off to his room.

Mr B did not pursue him. I give up, he thought. No matter which way this heap of shit slides, it is still a heap of shit.

His head throbbed and he could not see a way through. Fine, he thought. Let Bob's relationship with Lucy explode however they (or Mona) willed it. He was tired of chasing them all over the planet. In a very few days now, Bob would have to make his own decisions. He might as well get used to it now.

Mr B sighed. If he were honest, he'd have to admit that his own role in this bizarre tragicomedy seemed to have shrunk, leaving him more of a bystander than ever. Perhaps this was in preparation for his departure. Once he heard about his transfer, every single one of them could go to hell for all he cared.

But even as the thought came to him he knew it to be untrue.

If I didn't care, he thought, my head would not hurt. If I didn't care, my eyes would not ache and my gut would not churn and none of this idiocy would bother me. Indifference is the key, he mused, but I seem to have no talent for it. I care about Earth and all of Bob's tragic creations. I care about Estelle, and I care about Eck, he thought, though I cannot allow myself to think of him, for there is nothing I can do to reverse his fate. I care about Mona, despite a clear understanding of her faults.

And then a funny thought occurred to him, so funny that he began to laugh. And once he began laughing he could barely contain himself. How pathetic I am, he thought. I even care about Bob.

When next he looked up, Eck's friend was staring at him.

'Hello,' she said.

He pushed his spectacles back with one finger and smiled at her. 'I don't think we've been properly introduced.'

She held out her hand. 'I'm Estelle. My father won Eck in a poker game and is planning to eat him.'

Well, thought Mr B. She certainly gets straight to the point.

'Yes,' he said. 'It is a very sad state of affairs.'

She nodded.

'Have you spoken to your father?' Surely she, of all people, could change his mind.

Estelle nodded, and he thought he saw something dark flicker behind her eyes. Power flowed round her like a shield. He was interested to note that, despite her mild appearance, she was Hed's daughter.

'There's no progress to be made there,' she said carefully. 'But there may be another way. Only . . .' Her level gaze met his. 'I need help.'

Who doesn't, Mr B thought. 'I'm at your service,' said he. 'But . . . I feel I should tell you I don't expect to be here much longer.'

'Oh?'

'It's not exactly common knowledge . . . and of course it mustn't be.' He took a deep breath. 'I've resigned.' There, he thought. I've said it.

Estelle's eyes widened. He was interested to note that she was not, in fact, entirely unflappable.

'How soon will you go?'

Mr B shrugged. 'Very soon indeed. A matter of days.'

The colour rose in her pale cheeks. 'You're going to leave Earth to Bob?' Her distress nearly prevented her from speaking. 'What will become of it? He cares about nothing but himself.'

'And Lucy. The assistant zoo-keeper.'

'No,' said Estelle. 'That doesn't count. She's human.'

Was she right about that? Mr B removed his spectacles. 'I couldn't be more sympathetic to your concerns, but you must try to see it from my perspective. I've spent more millennia with Bob than I wish to contemplate, many thousands of years attempting to stem the gush of misery on this planet. And every minute of every day represents nothing to me but more failure.' He shook his head. 'I can no longer endure it. I cannot continue to assist him in this particular endeavour.'

Estelle looked at him, really looked, and saw everything she needed to see. Then she turned away and began to think. And, being an excellent thinker, she began to see a bigger picture, one informed by her travels and experience. One in which a whole raft of problems might slot together to form an elegant conclusion.

She looked back at Mr B, whom she found to be a most sympathetic individual. 'And Eck?' she said. 'He hasn't much time left either.'

He nodded. 'I will do what I can to help.'

39

'I want you to get rid of her.' Bob is back.

Which her, Mr B wonders. Not Lucy, surely?

'My mother. She's driving me insane. Get rid of her.'

Mr B is consumed with an irresistible urge to laugh. 'Get rid of your mother? How do you propose I do that?'

Bob does not answer. He stuffs an entire croissant into his mouth, hoping that his inability to speak will deflect attention from the fact that he has no intention of doing so.

Mr B shrugs. 'I couldn't get rid of her if I tried. She's indestructible. A universal force.'

The boy's face clouds over with annoyance. 'Well, then, *force* her to go away and stop ruining my life.'

'No can do, buddy boy. Your mother's your own problem. I'm as powerless in the matter as you are.'

Bob flushes with rage. 'But she listens to you,' he shouts. 'She likes you!'

'You're her son. She likes you more,' says he, sipping his coffee, unsure if the statement he has just made is true. 'Why don't you reason with her?'

'Hello? Have you *met* my mother? She's immune to reason.

She's made up her mind about Lucy, and who knows what she's plotting.'

'She is, of course, perfectly correct about Lucy.'

Bob's eyes roll back. For a moment, it looks as if his head might explode.

Mr B thinks. 'I could talk to her,' he says at last. 'But I should like something in return.'

'In return?' The boy looks genuinely nonplussed. 'Why should I do anything for you in return?'

'Because . . .' Mr B finishes his coffee and replaces the cup gently in the saucer. 'Because, if you don't, there's no deal.'

Bob's eyebrows shoot up. 'What? What are you talking about? Of course there is. There's always a deal.'

'Says who?'

'Says everyone. It's obvious. You have to. I'm the boss, you're not. You do what I say. End of story.'

'Ah. Now, you see, that is where you're wrong, technically speaking. In point of fact, my compliance is key to the execution of your desires.'

Bob chokes. 'Do you mean to say that if you don't *want* to do what I say you don't have to?'

Mr B nods.

'Since when?'

A shrug. 'Since always.'

Bob staggers to his feet, appalled, then sits down again with a crash. 'Why have you never mentioned this?'

'Why bother? My job is to comply with your wishes, so that's what I've done. But nothing actually *forces* me to do so.' Mr B pauses. 'It's what you might call a loophole.'

'*A loophole?*' Bob nearly screams the words. 'Are you

insane? If anyone's going to create a loophole around here, it's me. And this is not one!' He collapses in his chair.

'Indeed.' The older man sips his coffee.

Their eyes meet, and a current of something deeply unpleasant passes between them.

Bob has stopped chewing and looks as if he might cry. 'You don't care about me at all. No one cares about me except Lucy. Not even my own mother. Not even you.'

Lucy doesn't care about you, Mr B thinks. Not the real you, at any rate. She has no idea who – or what – you are. But I do. He looks away, and when he turns back, his expression is mild. 'Of course I care for you. Just as you care for me.'

Bob stuffs another piece of croissant into his mouth.

'So I suppose you'll be sorting out your most recent problems on your own, then.' Mr B dabs at his mouth with a large white linen napkin.

Bob stops chewing. 'Why not?' he says, gathering together what remains of his shredded dignity. 'I am God, after all. And I don't need you.'

'Good for you, that's the spirit.' Mr B rinses his cup in the kitchen, and returns, humming, to his desk.

40

A tap on the window of his bedroom wakes him from a deep and satisfying sleep, in which he is dreaming of doe-eyed virgins with budding breasts and silky skin ministering unto him with a variety of filthy acts. At the foot of the bed, the Eck tosses and turns uneasily.

Bob resents being awakened more than he can express.

'Go away,' he mutters, flinging the other arm out wildly, hoping to land a blow on whatever intruder dares to bother him. But the arm connects only with air, and the rapping continues, becomes louder, in fact, until he is forced to open his eyes and sit up and demand that whoever is making that awful racket should stop instantly or face the wrath of –

There is a splintering crash.

'Hello.' Estelle has stepped through the broken window and now stands at the foot of his bed. She looks larger than he remembers.

Bob gapes.

'I'm sorry to burst in on you this way, but I've come to take your Eck.' Her voice, despite being quite soft, hurts his ears.

With a little cry of joy, Eck scrambles towards her. Bob reaches out and grabs him by one ear. He yowls.

'Not so fast.' Bob maintains his grasp on Eck's ear. 'You can't just come here and take away my pet. He's got a reprieve, remember. Tell your father he'll have to wait for his dinner.'

Eck shrinks in terror.

Estelle becomes very still. 'Your pet will be gone for good in a matter of days if you continue to ignore his predicament.'

'I don't ignore him.' Bob is outraged. 'Just tonight I made him bring me some food, didn't I, Eck?'

Eck nods, looks from one to the other. He trembles with uncertainty.

'Release him, please.' Estelle's gaze is steely.

Bob hmphs with resentment, but he releases the Eck, who stands frozen to the spot. Estelle bends down and holds her arms out to him, but he no longer knows whom to trust.

From her bag, Estelle produces a cake and, instead of breaking off a piece, offers him the entire thing. He sways, torn between fear and the lure of the snack.

'Bad Eck!' shouts Bob. 'Stay!'

That seals it. The Eck scuttles over to Estelle, gingerly plucks the cake from her hands and allows her to pick him up as he eats. He settles into the crook of her arm.

Bob fumes. 'Put down my pet.'

'No.' She does not look at him.

'You'll regret it.' He is God.

She turns to go.

Bob mumbles furiously and pushes the hair out of his eyes. What gives her the right to so superior an attitude? He is frightened of Estelle but will not admit it, even to himself.

As she exits with his Eck, something snaps.

Bob closes his eyes and, with an enormous roar, brings the building down upon them all. It falls in on itself, a vast bouncing hole filled with filthy water and rubble. The collapse throws up a crashing wave that slams against the building opposite and turns back on itself in the narrow road. Like the casualties of a terrible disaster at sea, people scream and weep and bleed and drown, leaving dark stains on the surface of the water, along with the contents of their homes and bowels and skulls.

Well, thinks Bob, with satisfaction. I think that gives me the last word.

He turns to go, stepping carefully over the body of a young woman crushed in what is left of the stairwell. Surely it is time that he and Mr B found a new place to live in any case, maybe bigger, in a better neighbourhood, with more windows and a nicer view. He is considering the possibilities when a figure steps in front of him. It is Estelle. She is very much alive, but she holds the unconscious bloodied body of his pet.

'How could you,' she says, her voice icy with rage. 'How could you be so cruel? He's never done anything but serve you in the most humble manner. And this is how you repay him? *He* is not immortal.' Her voice rises only slightly, but the intensity of it causes him to tip backwards. 'You are so appallingly self-obsessed that you can't even manage to love your own pet. What kind of a God does that make you?' Her eyes flash with a fathomless whirling black fury.

Bob reaches out to Eck, but Estelle steps away.

'Don't you dare come near us.' Her voice is brittle as frozen steel. 'You don't deserve the loyalty of an Eck. You deserve *nothing*.' She stands very straight, could annihilate him with her gaze. '*You are nothing.*'

Bob transforms himself into a thick cloud of icy black gloom and seeps his way back home, to his and Mr B's new home, which looks more or less identical to their previous home with the exception of his bedroom, which is considerably smaller than before, and Mr B's, which is considerably larger.

'Did somebody say "help"?' Mr B looks up from his work.

'Yes, help. Please help me,' gabbles Bob, a miserable wretch-like version of his former self. 'Everything's gone wrong. Get rid of Estelle and my mother and I'll do whatever you like in return.'

Mr B peers at him thoughtfully. 'Well,' he says, 'I'll see what I can do. In exchange, I'd like you to sort out the weather.' He pauses, clears his throat and hands Bob the file marked W, for whales. 'And see what you can do about this.'

Bob's eyes widen.

'It's a big file,' admits Mr B. 'But this is your chance to do something grand and wonderful. Like you did in the beginning. Take it. Read it. Remind yourself why you're God.'

Bob accepts the file. His mouth is slightly open, his expression bleak.

Mr B watches him go. He has no idea what to think.

41

'Hello. May I sit down?'

Lucy moved her tray over to make a space.

'You look deep in thought. I'm not interrupting?'

'No, no. I know what you're going to say – I'm miles behind on my timesheets.'

Luke stuck a forkful of steaming noodles into his mouth. 'Ow-ow-ow, *hot*.' He made a face. 'We've abandoned timesheets for now.'

'Oh.'

He concentrated on his lunch, not looking at her. 'How's it going?'

Could it be a trick question? Lucy shrugged. 'Fine. I mean, we're overstretched, obviously. There are only four of us in today.' She bit her sandwich and chewed slowly, watching him.

He nodded. There was an awkward silence.

'Skype managed to get in.' She forced a smile.

'Yes. Of all people.' He could see now that she looked tired; the delicate tissue under her eyes bruised violet with fatigue. He fought an almost irresistible desire to trace the half-circles with his finger.

That look again. Of complicity. Lucy released his gaze a split second too late. Embarrassed, she turned away. 'She's not so bad if you tell her what to do.'

'Don't know when she finds time to work. She's slaving night and day on my horoscope,' he said. 'And the ley lines under the zoo. And the weather, of course. She's very tuned in, you know, to the paranormal.'

Lucy made her eyes huge and innocent. 'Anyone with an ounce of spirituality could, like, intuit that?'

Luke smiled. 'How's Bob?'

She blushed furiously. Nothing. She'd heard nothing. Why hadn't he called? Or come to see her? Had it meant so little to him? Had *she* meant so little? Was sex all he wanted? And the talk of love – was that nothing too? The sandwich in her throat turned to clay. She wanted to cry. 'I-I haven't known him very long.' Christ, she thought. I sound like an idiot.

'Ah. So it was love at first sight, then?'

'Oh, please don't.' She couldn't joke about it and scrabbled to change the subject, but came up with nothing. *Why hasn't he called?* Tears filled her eyes.

He peered at her, gently now. 'I'm sorry. It's none of my business.'

Lucy swiped at the tears with an angry hand. 'It's fine.'

'Don't mind me. I'm just jealous.' Luke's expression was almost tender.

Lucy looked up. Was he still teasing her?

He twirled up another forkful of noodles, blew on it this time, and then held it aloft, in tribute. 'Here's to a long and happy life together – for you and Bob.'

And the instant he said those words, Lucy knew, as if

staring into a particularly reliable crystal ball, that what Luke had wished for her would never come to pass. She felt the blood drain from her face.

He stopped chewing. 'I've said the wrong thing again.'

'No, no, no.' She turned away. 'Happy ever after. Right.'

Luke downed the last of his coffee and stood to go, a little awkwardly, adding as an afterthought, 'You don't know anything about a missing capybara, do you?'

Oh, Christ.

'Never mind. He probably just decided to go for a swim.' Luke's phone bleeped and he pushed back his chair, picking up his tray in one hand and waving a brief goodbye.

She watched him go, thinking how much her mother would approve of *him*. Gainfully employed. Tall. Nice looking. Possibly funny. No obvious mysteries – except why, after months of the silent treatment, he had suddenly turned nice.

Men were horrible, she thought. Hot one minute, cold the next. How could a normal person be expected to keep up with all the twists and turns . . .

Bob had seemed nice, too. Better than nice.

Oh, *damn the lot of them.*

By the time she made it home that night, she felt exhausted. Pouring a glass of wine, she flopped down on the sofa and tried not to think about Bob. Impossible. A minute later she was on her feet, pacing, furious, unable to settle.

She'd had it with waiting around for him to drop by with his little miracles, was tired of wondering how and when he'd appear next. It was time she saw him on her terms, asked what he meant by having sex with her and then disappearing. The bastard.

I can't stand any more of this, she thought, and in a wildly uncharacteristic gesture hurled her glass against the wall. From somewhere across the city a gigantic BOOM echoed the explosion of shards. It was mysterious, but strangely satisfying.

I must talk to him, she thought. If he won't get in touch with me, I'll go to his house. What have I got to lose?

She had his address and there was nothing to stop her dropping in on him. In fact, there had never been a reason not to visit him except, she realized now, how frightened she was of what she might find.

Navigating the city was difficult these days, but she walked as far as she could and then found a reasonably honest-looking water taxi to take her the rest of the way. It even had a little putt-putt motor, for which she agreed to pay extra.

'Some kind of incident in that neighbourhood,' said the driver without changing expression, after which he fell silent.

Incident? What sort of incident? By the time they arrived, the sun had disappeared over the horizon and though the sky was still light, the city below was nearly dark. And from fully half a mile away it became clear that something was wrong. Revolving lights in blue and red swept the dark water and the walls of adjoining buildings; police and rescue boats, filled with the injured wrapped in silver blankets, came past. Their little boat tossed left and right on the wake. At the end of Bob's road, puddles of floodwater appeared black in patches, and when Lucy dipped her hand in, it came up red. She recoiled in horror.

'What happened?' she asked, and a distraught woman

told her that a suspected gas explosion on Bob's street had caused an entire building to collapse. Debris floated everywhere – large pieces of furniture hung just below the surface, antimacassars and bedsheets pursued the boat in jostling competition to disable the little propeller. Lucy's driver rescued a bamboo curtain rod and used it to push debris away.

Lucy felt sick. Was it Bob's building? Was that why he hadn't called?

She stared at the terrible gap left by the explosion and then glanced along the street. Nine, ten, eleven . . . surely, this *was* number twelve. Her heart began to thump painfully and she wanted to howl with fear, but when she turned her attention to the next building, she exhaled, relieved. Number twelve. Still standing. But how strange. And the one that blew up? Number eleven and a half?

'Hello?' She directed her boatman further along and called across an open window. It wasn't exactly easy to drop in on someone unannounced in the middle of an emergency in the middle of a flood. She called louder. 'Hello!'

Indeed, the presence of a visitor seemed so unlikely that at first Bob wondered if he'd imagined it. He was hard at work on the whale problem, locked in his own world. His head hurt and he had reached no solution. He put his hands over his ears to block out the noise. What now? Why couldn't everyone leave him alone?

Three windows opened on to the street from the living room; to the right a fourth led to Bob's bedroom, to the left, a fifth opened out from the kitchen. Mr B's study and bedroom were at the back. The living room that Lucy scanned could have belonged to anyone. Was this the right place? Decorated in neutral colours with unobtrusive furnishings, it had the slightly impersonal look of a show apartment. Lucy peered past the mid-range modern furnishings (white L-shaped sofa, glass table, chrome-framed chairs) and could just pick out another room beyond. But no, this couldn't be right. Bob wouldn't live like this. He'd have books, African masks, animal prints. Interesting relics from his travels. She searched along the front of the building. It appeared to be the only flat on the first floor. Could it be? As she tried to knock again, the boat swung away from the wall and carried her along to the right.

It was harder to see into this room, which was darker, but she could make out a large bed, and a somewhat confusing variety of pictures on the walls. A huge poster of Michelangelo's *Creation of Man* faced off a naked woman astride a shiny Italian motorbike. Adam and God had eyes only for each other, but the girl with perfect golden buttocks stared over one shoulder seductively at Lucy, who stared back, perplexed.

And then she saw Bob. He looked damp and unkempt. She crouched in the boat, gripping on to his windowsill, watching him pace back and forth. He hesitated occasionally, stopping to tug at his hair or hold his hands over his ears. Through the window she could hear him making an odd noise, halfway between a growl and a moan.

She blinked at the scene, fighting waves of nausea.

The third time she called his name he looked up. She tried to smile at him, but he seemed disorientated, distressed. He looked like a madman.

'Bob?' She had to shout to be heard through the window.

He did not appear to recognize her.

'Bob? Are you OK? Why haven't you . . .?' She could not go on. He stared at her blank and wild-eyed. No. Not at her, through her.

The magnitude of her mistake choked her; she wished herself anywhere in the world but here.

'Please,' she said to the taxi driver. 'Please! Turn around, take me away from here.' As they began to back away, Bob seemed at last to see her. He ran to the window and threw it open, reaching for her.

She shrank away, trembling.

'Lucy!' His voice was hoarse, unnatural. 'What are you doing here?' Oh, Christ. He covered his face with both hands. Perfect. Estelle on his case. *And* his mother. And now Lucy, here. It wasn't that he no longer loved her, of course not – only, the timing was bad. Worse than bad. If he didn't sort out the whales, Mr B wouldn't get rid of his mother and Estelle. And as long as his mother and Estelle stuck around, the prospect of any happiness in his life with Lucy was doomed.

Bob tried to refocus on the Lucy he loved, the Lucy with whom he planned to spend forever. But he couldn't. His feelings had shifted. Not in the way Mr B had predicted, no . . . but, really, he was so distracted. And here on his own territory she seemed more of a nuisance than anything.

'Look!' He was shouting, though he didn't realize it. 'Look, you can't come in now. It's complicated. I have to do something about the whales, the fish, the oceans in general. I've got to save them. I might have an idea, but it's tricky; it's been a long time since I created anything this big, if you get my meaning, too long. Millions of years.' He laughed weirdly, wildly.

Oh my God, she thought. At first, it had seemed possible that his distress could somehow be related to the accident, or even his consulting job. But what sort of consulting required a person to save the 'oceans in general'?

Bob waved a hand at her dismissively. 'I can't explain, you wouldn't understand.' He rolled his eyes and waggled his head back and forth. 'It's all about the planet, blah blah blah. All part of a day's work. And anyway, don't you know?' He stopped, and began to laugh uproariously. 'I only rest on the seventh day.'

He's psychotic, she thought. Delusional. Her first impulse was to cry, but a stronger instinct told her it was not safe to remain here.

She turned to the taxi driver once more. 'Go,' she said. 'Go *now*.'

Bob continued to cackle; he seemed to have forgotten her altogether. His arms were waving now. He was muttering in what sounded like a foreign language, or a combination of languages, and his eyes had lost their focus.

She had lost her virginity to a madman. She wished she could have it back.

42

Laura Davenport was preoccupied. It had taken forever to convince herself that the responsible thing to do was to challenge Lucy about the strange young man she was seeing. Only now that she had determined to confront her, she could get no answer on Lucy's phone.

Lucy rarely left the house this early; perhaps she'd had to, on account of the weather? Laura left messages, waited an hour, and tried her at work. But the person who answered the phone at the zoo didn't seem to know anything about her whereabouts.

'Probably couldn't get here because of the weather? It's, like, a total nightmare?' As if to prove the point, a great crash of thunder echoed down the line.

'But she's not answering her landline. Or her mobile.'

'Wish I could help?' She could hear the shrug in the girl's voice. She sounded young. 'We're trying to sort out the animals. Though, between you and me, I'm pretty sure the rain is, like, nearly finished?'

Despite her anxiety, Laura was taken aback. 'How could you possibly know?'

'Tarots? I did a reading this morning and all signs are for, like, change?'

Laura put the phone down slowly. What an odd conversation. She shook the words out of her head, threw on her coat and grabbed the car key from a Chinese bowl by the front door. The engine sputtered at first but then caught, and she set off at speed, travelling half a mile before reaching an uncrossable ford. It was mere luck that a police barricade stopped her going forward, for she would have ploughed on regardless. She pulled up at the last moment and took out her phone.

'Bernard, oh, thank heavens you've picked up. I can't raise Lucy anywhere and I have such an awful premonition. I know it's terrible to ask when you're so overtaxed, but I really must get to her.'

He left immediately.

A trip that might have taken six minutes by car took nearly an hour. By the time he arrived, Laura was rigid with anxiety and, without a word, Bernard swept her off to Lucy's, following the motorway as best they could, dodging larger craft and makeshift pirate transport. Laura gripped the wooden thwart with bloodless hands, her eyes turned inward, as Bernard brought the boat expertly alongside Lucy's balcony. Laura slipped over the railings with surprising grace. She knocked loudly on the glass, falling back in relief when Lucy appeared at the window.

Laura folded her anxious daughter into a ferocious hug. 'I was so worried.' Her voice trembled. 'I phoned . . .'

'Flat battery.' Lucy pulled away, impatient.

In the corner of the room, Bernard waited for what came next, while Laura busied herself in the kitchen with the tea. As she handed a flowery mug to Lucy, the girl's composure sagged and her eyes overflowed. 'Oh! Oh!' she said, in a distressed bleat. 'Mother.' She began to weep.

Laura froze.

'He said he loved me.' Lucy wiped her eyes on her sleeve and took a deep breath, attempting to stem the flow of emotion without success. 'He said he wanted to marry me and be together forever.'

But, thought her mother, *but*?

'He said I was the only woman in the world for him.' She stopped and covered her face with her hands, choked and shaking with misery. 'I feel such an idiot.'

Laura put down the tea. She desperately wanted to approach her daughter, but didn't dare, for fear of inciting her ire. Instead, she tried to radiate sympathy from the spot. It was agonizing.

Lucy didn't move.

'Darling? Can you tell me?'

'It doesn't matter,' she said angrily. 'It's over.'

To hide her relief, Laura stepped forward and embraced her daughter. 'My poor darling. He's not worth weeping over. If he doesn't appreciate a girl like you . . .' But, even to her own ears, the words sounded quaint. What man ever warranted the tears shed on his behalf?

'It's fine.' Lucy struggled free of her mother's arms. 'You don't have to say all that.'

Hovering by the window, Bernard was the unwilling witness to this intimate scene. Laura saw him glance at his

212

watch. She crossed over to him and touched his elbow.

'I'm so sorry, Bernard. It's not what I expected.' She spoke softly, even laughed a little. 'Thank God.' She had imagined a bath full of blood, dismembered limbs, the awful dangle of feet. Now she could admit it.

'We had to come. And she's all right, that's the main thing.' Laura looked smaller than usual, and older. He felt an almost overwhelming urge to gather her up in his arms.

'Go, Bernard. A little heartbreak, that's all. Part of the human condition. It won't be the last time.' The look they shared spoke of the sympathy and wisdom of age, of its disappointments and yearnings, its habit of unacknowledged feelings. Without intending to, Laura took hold of Bernard's hand in both of hers and laced her fingers tightly through his. It was as good as an admission, and for a moment neither dared to move, except to run one soft thumb along one warm palm. In the future, both would think of the moment with doubt, wondering whether they had imagined the gesture.

Bernard kissed his tearful goddaughter on the cheek, buttoned his jacket against a sudden icy wind and left, nearly bumping into a ragged, distraught-looking youth perched on the ledge of a nearby building with his coat pulled up round his face. The boy muttered and growled at him, like a dog. One of the homeless deranged, Bernard thought. I should probably offer him a lift.

But he didn't.

43

Estelle has been a vigilant nurse. She is there when he blinks open his eyes and there again when he recovers enough to feel thirst. The water she brings in a glass tastes good. When she strokes his brow, her hand is cool.

She stays with him as he slips in and out of a feverish sleep; her voice, light and cool, falls around him like snow. She tells him stories of her plans in such a manner that he wants to survive.

Estelle holds him in her arms. His nose lies against the outside of her left breast and across her armpit, curling over her shoulder in a soft hook. She smells to him like linen and teacakes. Hour after hour she lulls him to sleep and lulls him awake again. He wonders if he has, after all, died. This is how he imagines heaven.

Eventually his wounds will heal. In the meantime, his feelings for her have knitted them together like two parts of the same bone.

Meanwhile, Bob has been thinking about the oceans until his brain feels wild and spinning and hot. He has managed to stop the rain; the city is already returning to normal. But sort out the whales? It is too much. He has tried, really he has, tried until he is nearly delirious with the effort. The rest of the world has become a blur; he is no longer conscious of anything beyond the turmoil inside his head.

Mr B does not seem to realize how hard it is for him to accomplish things on his own, he, who once created an entire world from nothing. He has not bothered trying to fix anything in a very long time. It seems he has forgotten how.

Hunched and miserable, he dozes off, dreaming of Lucy – beautiful, gentle, Lucy, beckoning to him with open arms and lips of ineffable softness. Oh, Lucy, Lucy! A terrible vision jolts him awake. *She came to find him and he sent her away.* Why? What had he been thinking? Now he must see her. The power of love courses through him, bolstering his resolve, spurring him on.

He arrives at Lucy's jittery and distraught, pauses on a nearby window ledge to calm himself. He breathes deeply, running dirty fingers through matted hair. His eyes are red with lack of sleep, his clothes ragged. He does not want to frighten her but cannot help the way he looks. The past few days have been dreadful.

'Lucy!' he cries, pounding on her window. 'Lucy, it's me!'

But the shutters are closed and locked and it is not Lucy who answers. 'Go away, or we'll phone the police and have you put away.' Lucy's mother's voice through the front door quivers with rage. 'We'll have you . . . flayed!'

Flayed? Bob frowns. Who would you hire to carry out a flaying in this day and age?

'Go away.' Lucy's voice is muffled but her pain penetrates wood and glass and pierces his heart. 'Please, go away. Go away, and never, ever come back.'

He hears a noise that might be a sob and then the other voice chimes in with unnecessary enthusiasm. 'You are lower than the lowest of the low!'

And the muffled retort: 'Thank you, Mother. I think I can handle this.' She thinks of the boy she thought she loved. He is not well. He needs help. But from her? No, not from her.

'What about our cottage by the sea?' he shouts through the door. With a pang, he remembers that there is no cottage by the sea. Though he can hardly be blamed for not sorting it out; life has been unusually demanding of late. 'Lucy? Lucy, my darling, my love, please, please, open the door.'

'Go away, you monster!' It is the other voice again.

Abruptly, it stops, and the noises within turn querulous. Then there is silence. He can imagine Lucy's mother hissing advice: *Don't say a word, it'll only encourage him.*

Bob is suddenly tired of acting human and materializes inside the flat. Lucy begins to scream. None of this is going the way he wishes it would. Lucy and her mother run from him, cowering. He hears the locking of the bathroom door, as if a locked door could make the slightest difference.

Their fear annoys him. It's just me, he wants to shout. Me, Bob!

He hears the sound of her fear, choking and gasping, and knows that what his mother and Mr B have been telling him all along is true.

'Lucy,' he whispers into the crease of the bathroom door. 'I thought we might be happy.' Tears choke him. On the other side of the door, Lucy squeezes her eyes shut in terror and prays.

*

At home, he sags against a wall, his heart heavy with despair. What becomes of him now is a matter of total indifference. He looks up.

'I'm sorry about your friend.' Estelle stares down at him. Her expression, as usual, is serene.

'Sorry?' He sounds peevish and wild. 'No problem! Sorry for what? The conspiracy to ruin my life? Never mind!' His rage and disappointment have found an object. Great jagged sheets of electricity flow off him.

Estelle does not appear to be frightened. She does not, in fact, appear moved in any way. As if embarrassed, the electrical field begins to fade. It fizzes a little, hisses, then stops altogether.

Estelle waits. She watches him. 'You haven't asked about Eck.'

Bob glares, furious. 'Eck? Of course I haven't asked about him. Why should I? Has he asked about me?'

Estelle considers Bob. It is not that she feels any particular responsibility for Earth, but she finds it impossible to imagine a world ruled by such a God, especially once Mr B has gone. Bob without Mr B is unthinkable. Mr B, at least, does what he can. He does *something*, despite the perfectly accurate sense that it is not enough.

'Eck is due to be eaten in two days. Have you thought about how to help him?'

Bob casts about, desperate. *Eck?* He's supposed to save *Eck?* But who's going to save *him?* He tears at his hair; his head threatens to explode. It's all too much. Lucy, his mother, Estelle. The whales, Mr B. Eck.

'I can't save Eck. I have to sort out the oceans. The whales.

In order to get rid of my mother.' He slumps, waves a hand at her, feebly. 'It's too complicated to explain.'

Estelle looks at him, at the gaunt face and staring eyes. Her brain ticks over. His mother? The whales?

I can't cope, thinks Bob. I may be God, but I can't cope. Let me go to bed and stop thinking; let me close my eyes and ears, curl up in bed and sleep. I need comfort, he thinks peevishly. Where's my Eck?

Bob misses him.

Estelle's brows draw together. A muscle in her neck tenses. Once more, she attempts to move the players around the board in her head, like chess pieces. She will know when they have all assumed their proper squares.

Bob kicks the wall of his bedroom. He feels beleaguered, wrong-footed, oppressed. Why should he care about that miserable penguiny stump? What has Eck ever done for him? Other than run errands and do what he's told, which is what he's paid to do in any case. OK, not paid. None of it makes him worthy of *love*, for pity's sake. He's only an Eck, and not even one of the better ones. How dare she look at him that way. How *dare* she make him feel guilty.

Estelle takes her leave, thoughtful.

He is alone, pacing, distressed. And then all at once outraged pride pricks him, and his energy comes together in a surge. He needs to feel powerful again, needs to feel like a god. His face is hot, his brain buzzing with the fever of creative possibilities; suddenly, a job that appeared insoluble has myriad solutions, each bolder and more dangerously unconventional than the last. Whales. Oceans. His powers may be rusty from lack of use, but a stubborn resolve overtakes him. In a great flash of resentment and fury he sets something in motion. A terrible noise like the sucking of a whirlpool seems to emanate simultaneously from the very centre of the Earth and the outermost reaches of the galaxy.

Something glorious is born.

There, he thinks, collapsing on to his bed, exhausted. There. Now what?

44

Today is the first day of the rest of my life, thinks Mr B.

Nothing that happens on Earth is any longer his problem. He clutches the envelope; inside are details of his new job. Without pausing, he rips it open. First time through he skims, searching for key words.

Years of valued service . . . creativity, enthusiasm and skill . . . our deepest admiration . . . not toiled without notice . . . in recognition of the highest standards . . .

A warmth flows through him, a buzz of happiness unlike any he has ever known. Perhaps all the pain and misery have been worthwhile, just for the sweetness of this moment. What bliss to be acknowledged at last. He feels like singing, skipping for joy.

He jumps to page two. There is a description of his next job, '*as a reward for sterling performance*'. Oh, happiness upon happiness! He knows the planet; it is one of the best – sane and orderly, with an ancient structure, a perfect climate, a wise and contented population. He will be top God, sole God, with a full support staff that he imagines will prove entirely unnecessary. It seems wondrously, impossibly perfect.

Returning to his desk, Mr B experiences a temporary setback at the sight of his files spilling in heaps on every surface. This is the usual state of things, but he sees it with the eyes of a man surveying a place for the last time. So many petitions, so many prayers that will remain unheard unto eternity. Perhaps once he is gone, Bob will rise to the occasion.

Perhaps.

Perhaps (despite the accolades he now has in writing), perhaps he has not managed to fulfil the conditions of his job so well after all. Is he at fault? Has he failed to carry out the responsibilities that are within his control?

'*Highest standards . . . sterling performance . . .*'

His heart, which has been beating in frantic rhythm for hours, abruptly slows. The heaviness to which, over the years, he has become accustomed, returns to his limbs and for a moment he thinks he may sink to the floor. A pain at the centre of his being increases, radiating down both arms, up into his neck and jaw and head, down his trunk and both legs. He feels as if he is made of lead. If he did not know better, he would imagine that he is having a stroke.

'*Valued service . . .*'

How can he leave all of this behind? How will Bob alone take responsibility for Earth? At least he has managed, over the years, to satisfy the occasional request, reverse the fortunes of one in a thousand, one in a million, in ten million. At least he has *tried*. He has cared, genuinely cared, for the poor unfortunates created in the headlong rush of Bob's indifference, those destined to live out their fates in succeeding doomed generations, ad infinitum. He has cared for them as individuals as well as en masse. He has saved a few, eased some suffering, diverted a massacre where he could. One or two mothers' hearts have offered him thanks, despite the infinite number who have wept oceans of tears and cursed Bob's indifference.

His head is bowed; he half leans on his desk.

It is he, not Bob, who cares for this world.

Bob is not, and never has been, fit to rule. He is a cog. A boob. A cur.

He is no God.

If there even is such a thing as God, thinks Mr B. If there is such a being, it cannot be Bob.

He hesitates, and all at once a realization explodes in his brain like a bomb. He groans, gripping the desk to avoid falling.

Why has he never seen it before? *The obviousness of it.*

With purest clarity he realizes that Bob is not the God to whom the multitudes direct their entreaties. Bob is not the all-merciful, the all-seeing, all-knowing deity of grace and wisdom and compassion. If there is such a being, it is not the indifferent, underage parent of this world, the thoughtless creator. It is the *other*, the one who has struggled day after day to make things better, to answer a few prayers, right a few wrongs, who has suffered along with his planet and tried to fix things, in however small a manner, to change a detail here and there for the good of mankind, for the creatures, for all who suffer and long for a better life.

No. Bob is not God.

He is.

45

The fourteenth of July dawns full of promise: crystalline air, sharp colours, the edges of all things precisely defined. The rain has stopped and already pavements and roads have begun to re-emerge from beneath the floodwaters. The inhabitants of Bernard's church have returned home. Lucy can use her front door. No comets or balls of lightning trouble the sky. It is not raining frogs.

Earth looks ravishing.

It is dawn, and for the first time in weeks, Luke allows himself a lie-in for a few minutes after the alarm goes. It is his birthday, and nearly all the news is good. Through the window, he can already see that it has the makings of a beautiful day. The sky is clear, the land dry, the eerie reflections have gone from his walls. Light pours in through the tall glass window; he moves his face into a patch of sun.

He would like to wake up with someone, a woman worth crawling out of the warmth for. On a morning such as this, he would pad through to the kitchen to put the coffee on, present it to her as an offering. He would happily suffer the cold floor beneath his feet in exchange for the happiness of returning to bed for a few minutes to drink coffee and talk.

It has been nearly three years since his last relationship and the thought of it no longer fills him with bitterness. He chose his turret in a spirit of self-denial, he now thinks. Locking himself off from the world. He laughs at himself. Such a princess. Perhaps he has had enough of exile.

Below him in the city, on a wooden bench, Mr B sits, deep in thought.

All these years of service, based on a misunderstanding. He has left it to Bob (Bob the immature, the pathologically inept) when really it was his responsibility. What peculiar instinct for deference led him to this place?

He sits motionless for a very long time, until the feeling ebbs a little. It is no longer relevant. His contribution has been recognized and any minute now he will be off to greener pastures. Slowly he lifts his head and straightens his back, heaving a deep sigh. But he is not alone.

The man beside him is a decade or two his junior, a bit rumpled, peering at him gently through tortoiseshell glasses and clutching a china mug full of coffee. The man has a kind, wry demeanour and an air of knowing the pain of the world.

Mr B hasn't seen him arrive.

'Dry at last,' Bernard says, smiling. 'Hallelujah.'

Mr B turns away, embarrassed by his red-rimmed eyes.

Bernard's expression turns to one of concern. 'It's the weather, you see. Such a relief. But you've obviously . . . had a bad day? I'm terribly sorry.'

Mr B shrugs. 'It's not your fault. It's the job.'

'Mine too,' Bernard says cheerfully, his fingers moving unconsciously to his dog collar. 'Bloody business, religion. Don't know what bastard thought it up.'

Mr B looks at him. Sighs. 'Someone too young and too stupid to think it through properly. Someone so indifferent to life and death he thought it didn't matter.'

Bernard laughs, a little anxiously. 'Well, that would certainly explain it.'

'It's not right. Mortality is a terrible notion.' Mr B looks up at Bernard and lowers his voice, conspiratorially. 'It's not like this everywhere, you know.'

Bernard is not sure what sort of answer is required. He has begun to suspect that the man on the bench – despite his sympathetic face and manner – may be mad.

They sit in silence, watching an elderly man creep carefully along the pavement beside his slow-moving dog.

'How old do you suppose you have to be,' muses Mr B, 'not to mind dying?'

Bernard has not yet figured out how to make his escape. His profession requires a sympathetic response, and he does, after all, feel some genuine sympathy for this man and his mental-health problems. 'One hopes,' he says, 'after a long life, surrounded by loving family and the memory of good works . . .'

'That it might not seem such a bad prospect?' Mr B frowns. 'Now, you see, I think that's untrue. The occasional person genuinely doesn't mind. But most do.' He removes his spectacles and begins cleaning them on his handkerchief. 'Something about eternal nothingness really rocks the boat.'

Bernard chokes a little on his coffee and Mr B studies his face, bemused.

'Don't tell me that you, of all people, believe in God?'

Bernard shrugs apologetically. 'It tends to go with the job.'

'Yes, of course . . . and I don't mean to presume. But, *really*. What sort of god could you possibly manage to worship?' Mr B shakes his head. 'If ever a place were devoid of wisdom and guidance, this is it.' He peers at Bernard. 'Surely.'

The two men pause to watch the emergence of life around them, as people stretch their legs on dry ground for the first time in weeks: mothers guiding toddlers, entwined couples, slouching teenagers with skateboards. A man in an expensive suit tears bits off his sandwich and throws them to the ducks; a young woman shouts into her mobile phone.

'Just look at them trundling along pretending that cataclysmic nothingness isn't waiting for them just round the bend. I watch them sometimes and I think that it doesn't really matter how much I worry about them. It's all over so fast. A bit of suffering – an entire lifetime, even. It's nothing, really.' He pauses. 'In the greater scheme of things, they may as well be fruit flies. So what if no one answers their prayers? Poof! Wait a minute or two, and your problem is gone. Dead. Buried. Forgotten.'

Bernard glances around to see if they are being observed.

'I don't mean to shock you.' Mr B looks sorrowful. 'You strike me as a man who's seen most of what's shocking in life already.'

'Yes, but . . .'

'I know. It's not easy. Of course the whole concept's wrong. An expiration date on life?' Mr B blinks. 'Still. What's done is done.' He replaces his spectacles carefully, hooking the arms round first one ear then the other.

When Bernard stands up, the other man looks suddenly

as if he might cry. 'Don't run off, please. I'm sorry. I talk too much.'

Bernard sits. 'Do you think the strange weather is finished? At least we could be thankful for that.'

Mr B thinks about it. 'Of all the things happening today, yes, I suppose we can thank God for that. But who whipped up all the chaos in the first place? Him, in his infinite self-indulgence. So he buggers the place up, and maybe, sometimes, if he can be bothered, he stops us all from drowning in the aftermath.' He lowers his voice and leans in to Bernard. 'The whole construct is wrong, don't you see?'

Bernard looks puzzled. 'Sorry. Which construct, exactly?'

'Creation. Man, animals, the whole kit and kaboodle. Far too rushed, no follow-through, no consultation.' His head droops. 'Mistake after mistake. This fool of a God lacked the experience not only for creation, but for humility as well. So he slaps it all together in a few days and goes to bed thinking he's a genius.' Mr B shakes his head. 'The result –' his hand sweeps in an expressive arc – 'is this.'

Bernard perches on the edge of the bench, blinking at Mr B.

'OK, it doesn't look so bad today. But just you wait. Some awful new thing will begin any minute. It always does.' The older man shrugs. 'It's not cruelty, you see. It's thoughtlessness. Negligence.' He looks away and his face sags. 'Who knows,' he says softly. 'Perhaps even a lack of clarity as to the nature of his responsibility.'

Churning in Mr B's brain is a great stinking stew – of faith, commitment and love in the face of indifference, betrayal, despair. The world is not just full of suffering – it is full of perversity, of things that go horribly wrong more or less at random. For the hell of it.

'Sometimes,' he says, 'I don't understand how we go on.'

From a long habit of sympathy, Bernard places a reassuring hand on his shoulder. 'We go on because we have no choice.'

Mr B stares at Bernard with his deep sad eyes and sighs. 'Perhaps the way to proceed is to think of life on Earth as a colossal joke, a creation of such immense stupidity that the only way to live is to laugh until you think your heart will break.' He looks upwards to the branches, rich with summer green, stares through them to the sky beyond.

There is a catch in Bernard's voice. 'What you say makes my position untenable.'

'It is,' says Mr B with infinite tenderness. 'So is mine. So is everyone's.'

Mr B does not see his companion go. The next time he looks up, he is alone – still with the letter in his hand, the answer to his prayers.

After a time, he picks himself up and walks slowly home, clutching his future tightly to his chest.

'I should be happy,' he thinks.

46

Mr B enters this place for what must surely be the last time, followed closely by Mona.

'Hello, darlings!' She leans down and kisses Bob, who swats at her with one apathetic hand. He has spent the night huddled in the dark at the bottom of his wardrobe, thinking of Lucy and hoping the world would come to an end before dawn.

It will certainly come to an end for Eck, who is today due to be served up to Emoto Hed, lightly sautéed in butter and topped with a delicious peppercorn sauce.

Mona helps herself to a large glass of champagne. She hands another to Mr B, who puts it down.

'You're looking peaky, my darling,' says Bob's mother, reaching to feel God's forehead with the back of her hand.

'That's because my life is ruined.' Bob coughs and shudders, every muscle cramped and aching from his night on the dusty cupboard floor.

'Oh, dearest, I am sorry.' She frowns for an instant, then beams. 'But never mind that now.' She refills her empty glass.

Bob rolls off the large, L-shaped sofa and crawls over to Mr B. 'Could I speak with you for a moment, alone?'

The older man follows him out.

'I've done it.'

Mr B looks down at him, surprised. 'You have?'

'Yes. But just FYI, when I requested that you get rid of my mother, I didn't also require you to get rid of the only girl in the world I ever loved.'

'Lucy?' Mr B is somewhat bemused by so many turns of events. The safest course of action seems to be to say nothing.

'And, by the way, my mother is still around.' Bob is too dispirited to continue. With the last dregs of his energy, he crawls back to the sofa, pulls himself up on to one end and closes his eyes. The final image to imprint itself upon his waking eyeball is a fish.

Estelle, with her usual air of quiet resolution, has arrived accompanied by a nervous and much thinner Eck. The air of doom surrounding him is palpable. Mona has temporarily disappeared, perhaps to fetch more champagne. Mr B takes the seat beside Estelle and places one hand on Eck's sad, snuffling nose.

'I promised Bob I'd get rid of Mona,' he says.

She turns to look at him. 'I know,' she says.

Another mystery, thinks Mr B.

Outside in the world, a murmur has begun, rapidly increasing in volume. Mr B is first at the window. Estelle is next; they stare, transfixed. Mona crowds in, still clutching her champagne. She begins to laugh, clapping one hand over her mouth like a delighted child.

They all turn to look at Bob, who sleeps so deeply he could be dead.

It is a miracle. There are hundreds of them. Thousands. They hover just above tree level, basking in the warm sun. They are rising, each at a different pace. In the early moments they lie still, as if stunned by lightness. One shudders, like a dog, and lowers his tail – an experiment. He flows upwards towards the clouds, cautious at first, his great bulk light as air. Another joins him, and another.

There are too many, now, to count. They are big and small, in all shades of black and grey and green and fawn and mottled blue, giant baleens, majestic orca, sperm whales, humpbacks, grey whales, porpoises, pilots, beaked and minke whales. By the time the last ones have floated free of their inky dank soup, the leaders have risen to the height of a mast, a mountain, an aeroplane. Some swoop together like birds, birds of unimaginable size and bulk, their smiling mouths ajar. They click and twitter and boom out their gratitude, the sweetness of joy rumbles up from the depths of each gigantic gorge.

It is not just the whales who have learned to fly.

The other creatures of the oceans rise up too: great electric eels, whole shimmering shoals of silvery minnows, giant tuna, delicate transparent jellyfish, stingrays flapping their prehistoric wings, squid the size of luxury cars. The sky is crowded now, the faces of observers transfigured with ecstasy and fear. Mr B feels as if he has returned to the enchantment of that first time, when Bob created all that the waters brought forth abundantly.

Only this time, they are brought forth abundantly into the sky.

Wherever the great whales have struggled against annihilation, they rise. They frolic in the sky.

Estelle holds out her hand. A sardine evades her fingers with a flick of its tail. On the street below, everyone stares upwards. They have poured out of homes and schools and shops; they lean out of windows and doorways. They stand on balconies, gawping, astonished. The spectacle is so extraordinary that no one looks away. Men and women of all ages, children, babies, dogs and cats – everyone stares, faces turned to the sky.

Bob stirs. Opens one eye. *See?* says his expression. *I did what I said I'd do.* A second later he is unconscious again.

With tears in his eyes, Mr B looks at what Bob has wrought. It is miraculous, extraordinary, yes. But *a solution?* How will this solve his problem? What will happen next? He wants to shake Bob, demand to know what he was thinking, require him to return things to the way they were, to fix the oceans *properly, for God's sake.*

He looks at Bob and sees a hopeless callow schoolboy, selfish and lazy, obsessed with sex. But can he deny that there is also the strange energy, the flashes of brilliance, the miracles? Bob doesn't plan or consider consequences, but once in a while, when he puts his mind to it, he achieves magnificence. And then, a minute later, the vast tangled mountain of chaos reveals itself.

Bob blinks awake. He registers Mr B's gaze and in return sees only what he might become, and most dreads.

Around the world in every place without hope or light, the people stand, faces upturned with wonder. For a brief instant in the long and painful history of the planet, wars stop, blood feuds are forgotten, no one is murdered or desperate or sad. The entire world hesitates, uncertain and amazed. Perhaps, some think, the Red Sea really did part. Perhaps stone tablets truly did come down from the sky.

If whales can fly, surely more miracles are possible? Tomorrow another; the day after, another?

And maybe, thinks Mr B, before it all goes horribly wrong (for he feels certain that the world has witnessed a moment, nothing more), he can do something about the seas, so that when the creatures return home their lives will be better.

When their lives are better, so is his. That is where he differs from Bob.

What am I? he wonders. I am the one who bullies and prods, who cajoles and begs and pleads. I am the one with the files and the lists and the knowledge of life and death. I am the one who yanks Bob out of bed to do what needs to be done. I am the brain and the conscience of Bob; what is Bob without me? What am I without Bob, he wonders.

He looks at Estelle, who looks back at him with eyes that are calm and cool and kind.

They will soon know.

47

Emoto Hed has arrived with his chef. The expression on his face is grim. He suspects diversions, is impatient with the peculiar behaviour of the fish. Mona tries to smile. She turns to Mr B; panic boils in her head. Get it over with, she seems to be saying. She will not be safe until the transaction is complete.

Fish swim past the windows.

Bob is no longer asleep. He slouches beside Mr B, who has placed the transfer document face down upon the table. Beside Mr B stands Estelle. She holds the injured Eck in her arms, his nose on her shoulder. Silent tears trickle softly to the floor.

Estelle glances down at the document. She looks again. Blinks. What she sees causes her eyes to open very wide, to forget, for an instant, the fate of the Eck.

Hed's chef sharpens his butcher's knife against a well-used sharpening steel. *Swoosh, swoosh, swoosh.* The noise is sickening. Something dreadful is about to happen here, while outside, fish continue to swim through the air. Despite the miserable drama unfolding before them, the entire company hesitates briefly as a gigantic blue manta ray performs a series of swooping slow somersaults across the windows of the flat. For twenty seconds (or is it twenty years?) they all turn to gaze at the afternoon sky.

But now Emoto Hed nods to indicate readiness. His chef prises the Eck from Estelle's arms. She barely seems to notice.

For the first time, the assembled cast can see his injuries, the terrible bruises, unhealed gashes, the great lump on the side of his head. He sports a heavy bandage on one arm. Emoto Hed looks appalled.

'You expect me to eat *that*?'

The chef whispers in his ear. His finished meal will show no sign of the creature's flaws; any irregularities in the meat will disappear beneath the silky sauce. The chef squeezes and prods poor Eck, nodding and making mental notes for marinating and cooking times. At last, he raises the knife, tests it carefully with his thumb and positions it just in front of Eck's throat, planning the depth and the angle of his cut.

'Stop.' It is Estelle.

The colour rises in Hed's face, which begins to twist with rage. Mona shrinks, thinking of his terrible power, of everything that is at stake. But Estelle, unfazed, takes a step forward. She stays the knife by placing one firm hand on the chef's arm.

'I offer Mona,' she says in her clear soft voice. 'In lieu of the Eck.'

Hed looks intrigued. 'To eat?'

Mona gasps and collapses.

'If you like,' says Estelle calmly. 'But it would be a waste.

Alive, she will play cards with you day and night and amuse you in a thousand different ways. She is extremely beautiful and will make an excellent companion, although she did lie to you most shamefully about Ecks being delicious. Didn't you, Mona?'

Mona's eyes flicker open. From her position on the floor the assembled company all appear to be gazing down at her. Is there a right answer to this question? One that won't inspire Hed to convert her to a long thin scream of eternal agony?

Hed looks from one to the other, from the odd little damaged penguiny thing to the voluptuous golden goddess.

'So he is *not* the most delicious creature in nine thousand galaxies?' Hed's fury threatens to bring down the ceiling.

'Not exactly,' whispers Mona at last. Though secretly she is thinking that the one *she* ate was the most delicious in at least two or three thousand galaxies.

What follows is the most ominous pause in nine thousand millennia. The room itself seems to tremble.

At last Hed speaks. 'Well,' he says, and shrugs. 'If I can't eat the Eck, I'd only have to throw it away.' He looks at Mona with an expression that is not a great deal more pleasant than a threat, and before she can react he leans down to take her arm. With a sound like a great inhalation of breath, they disappear.

Bob glances at Mr B. The fish are saved and his mother is gone. Things are looking up.

Only one question remains.

With a flourish, Mr B lifts the authorization for his new job from the table. He holds it at arm's length for all to see.

Closing his eyes, he imagines the pleasure of freedom from Earth, life on his orderly new planet, how happy he will be.

'Ahem.' In time-honoured tradition, he taps a knife on Mona's champagne glass. 'I have an announcement to make.' He speaks to what remains of the assembly, which is, in truth, a bit of a disappointing audience: Bob, Estelle, Eck. And Emoto Hed's chef, who looks uncomfortable. A guest at the wrong party. 'I am afraid I shall be leaving you.'

'Off you go then.' Bob rolls his eyes.

'For good.'

'You're leaving Earth?' Bob's mouth drops open. 'No you're not. I won't allow it.'

'I'm afraid it's a done deal.'

Bob's voice booms with the power of outrage. '*I AM GOD. YOU CAN DO NOTHING WITHOUT MY PERMISSION.*'

'Terribly sorry, but technically speaking I'm afraid that's incorrect. My resignation has been accepted, and I have received transfer orders to a new planet. Quite a beautiful planet, in fact.' Mr B radiates bliss. This is his moment, the one he has imagined over and over, year after year, millennium after millennium.

Bob's face has gone purple with fury. He shrinks to the size of a button and expands like a huge balloon.

Estelle stands very still. Watching.

Mr B continues: 'I hope you will not consider me immodest if I quote from this letter: *In recognition of your sterling service in the face of insurmountable odds, etc., etc., etc., exceptional forbearance combined with creativity of the highest order, we are pleased to offer you –*' he skims down

– '*with our highest admiration . . . effective immediately.*' Overcome with the emotion of the moment, he wipes tears away with the back of his hand. 'I shall miss you all, and trust you to carry on, without me, the job I sought to do, and to remember in my name that there is much to accomplish on Earth, despite what often appears to be the most hopeless burden of woe . . .'

'La la la la la la!' Bob has closed his eyes, placed a finger in each ear and begun to sing, loudly. Hed's chef wanders off to the kitchen to rifle through the pantry cupboards, searching for something for lunch. Only Estelle and Eck attend Mr B now. Estelle's pure brow is slightly creased, but she smiles at him with tender sympathy. Eck's eyes have grown heavy. They close.

When there is no one left to witness them, Estelle gently takes the papers from him. With exquisite tact, she turns them over. Her finger slips down across the writing on the back of the envelope until it comes to the address. The addressee. Her finger rests long enough for Mr B to read the name carefully, something he has not done before.

He gasps. It cannot be. Staggering a little, he groans, grabbing on to the windowsill. Then he clamps his eyes shut; his entire body shivers violently.

Bob is suddenly alert. What's this? He removes his fingers from his ears. What new development is this?

Estelle hands the transfer papers to Bob, who scans them quickly. His petulant lip quivers, his eyes widen. He frowns, confused. When the truth finally dawns on him, he grins and whoops.

'Me!' he shrieks. 'The transfer is for me! I'm the genius!'

He jabs his finger at the paper. 'Me! Me! Look! It says so right here in black and white!' His voice rises. 'I am king of the gods, the best, the bravest! I'm the dog's bollocks; I'm the one with the fabulous new job! Hello? Would you like to see my *promotion*? *My* promotion? Who's the clever one, now? Me! *Exceptional forbearance and creativity of the highest order*? Me! *Sterling service in the face of insurmountable odds*? Me! *I'm* the one who gets to leave.' He begins to dance around the room, tucking in his chin, pumping his arms, lifting his knees and chanting: 'New plan-et! New plan-et! New plan-et!'

When Mr B opens his eyes once more, he is calm. He exhales a long hiss of breath. Estelle puts her hand on his arm. Her expression suggests that this is not so bad an outcome as it might seem.

'What about Lucy?' Mr B cannot resist the temptation to ask.

Bob's face drops, but only for an instant. 'I'll go and fetch her! I'll take her with me!' he cries.

They all freeze. And then Mr B exercises his first genuine act of earthly omnipotence. For an instant he concentrates very hard.

There is a hollow *boom* and quite suddenly, Bob is gone. One moment he stands among them. The next moment, poof! Nothing. Silence. A long silence.

'Well,' Mr B says at last, very softly, with an air of bemusement.

Estelle smiles at him, the most admiring of smiles. 'Well done,' she says.

Outside the window, the fish continue to swim through

the air. I have my work cut out for me, he thinks. Cleaning up after Bob, after his idiot inspirations, the ones that everyone thinks are so brilliant but which achieve precisely nothing. Mr B wonders how much time he has before the fish begin to die and fall from the sky, to smack and kill people on the way down, and then to lie and rot and stink in their hundreds of thousands and create a public health hazard of such proportions that the Black Death will seem as insignificant as a sore toe.

In the morning, he will think of all that must be done. He will go to his desk, push aside the piles of prayers that await him and return the fish to the seas. But right now, something far more urgent requires his attention. He turns to Estelle.

'Will you stay?' he asks, a little tentatively.

'Of course,' she says.

Of course. His heart soars.

For now, this makes him God enough.

48

Luke catches the bus to work. Like everyone else, his eyes remain glued to the sky – to the glorious spectacle, the strangeness, the inversion of everything he has always expected. The miracle is only a few hours old, and he cannot imagine a time when it will appear less magical, less hopeful than it does now.

I wonder what will happen next, he thinks, impressed and a little frightened by the spectacle. He would like to have stayed in his tower to watch the world reveal its next miracle. It is difficult for him to contemplate a continuation of real life, but there are animals to be cared for. An image of Lucy appears to him, as it has begun to do nowadays when he thinks of . . . almost anything. Above him, beautiful flashes of fishes fly.

Damn. He's missed his stop and the bus continues down to the bottom of the hill. When it stops again, he can see the aqua concrete walls that contain the penguin pools up the long slope above him. He leaps off the bus and begins to walk briskly uphill, feeling the stretch in his Achilles tendons and the backs of his knees. The day is clear and fresh, and, despite the unexpected climb, he feels optimistic, particularly when he sees Lucy (*ah, to feel the perfect synchronicity of the planet, if only for an instant!*) walking ahead of him. If he hurries, he will catch her up. *Whoever would have thought?* he will say to her, and then, *But why not? We are living in an age of miracles!*

The hill is steep and he begins to run. She stops when he says her name. He leans on her shoulder for a second to get his breath back.

'What a weekend!' he says to her.

Lucy shakes her head, her face transfigured by grief. 'I never want to think about it ever again as long as I live.'

'But the fish!' protests Luke, wrong-footed by the strength of her unhappiness. 'The fish are magic!'

Lucy thinks of the boyfriend she imagined she had and all that she is unable to understand. Who is Bob? What did he mean about fixing the oceans? And the strange, awful behaviour of the fish? A coincidence?

Luke reaches out his arm and snatches a tiny wriggling perch from the air. He holds it tickling in his hand for a heartbeat, grasps Lucy's wrist and places the fish in her palm, folding her fingers gently round it. Despite herself, she giggles and tosses it up into the sky. It swims off.

She sighs. 'Yes, the fish are magic. A great and terrible magic.' The moment is over. Her face turns blotchy and her eyes blink rapidly. She turns away so he won't see, and they walk in silence till they reach the gates, show their employee passes and are clicked through the turnstile.

Out of delicacy, he pretends not to notice her distress, but he keenly desires to look into her eyes and state with conviction that all will be well and all manner of things will be well.

A flash of jealousy, triumph and righteous ire rises up in him, and at the same time he feels a great rush of gratitude to Bob, for being so obviously the wrong man.

She turns away from him, but he is quicker. He takes her arm. 'I found your capybara,' he whispers close to her ear. 'He set up camp on a little island half a mile away. Happy as Larry. A bit hungry, maybe. Pleased to be home.'

Lucy's face transforms and lightens, quick as a child's. 'Oh, clever you,' she cries. For an instant her unhappiness evaporates. It will return, but for now she throws her arms round him, wondering how it is possible that she is doing such a thing. The sun, which has already gilded the edges of the day, seems to settle on the two of them like a kiss.

He pulls free and grabs her hand, his brain struggling to retain the brief imprint of her body on his. He experiences a moment of sudden, glorious clarity and breaks into a trot, pulling her along behind him. By the time they reach the enclosure she is laughing. He does not let go of her hand. And so they stand, while the impossible fish float overhead, gazing at Lucy's capybara and (a little unbelieving) at each other, wondering at the state of miracles.

They are flooded with hope.

More books by the
award-winning

meg rosoff

How I Live Now
'Timeless and luminous' OBSERVER

Just in Case
'Intelligent, ironic and darkly funny'
TIME OUT

What I Was
'A wonderful, captivating writer. 5*****'
DAILY TELEGRAPH

The Bride's Farewell
'It's already a classic' SUNDAY TIMES